"I don't think this, ah, friendship is good for my grandmother,"

Lenore told Steven with a strained smile. "I mean, she isn't particularly experienced with men, and, well, she's been alone a long time...."

There was a sadness in her voice that had a surprisingly potent effect on him. He shifted restlessly. "So why do you feel she might be susceptible to the lure of moonlight and soft music?"

Lenore moistened her lips with her tongue and swallowed hard. When she spoke, her voice had a soft, ethereal quality. "Loneliness is a bleak companion. Sometimes, at night, the ache begins, an emptiness that screams out for fulfillment. There's this incredible longing to see desire in a man's eyes and feel the heat of his passion...to be cherished again...and to be loved."

Steven's mouth went dry and he shivered. Unconsciously or not, Lenore had just described with stunning power the depth of her own desire. The realization took his breath away.

Dear Reader,

It's July, and at Silhouette Romance we have the perfect accompaniment to a day at the beach or a lazy afternoon in the backyard—six fabulous love stories that bring together the best possible happy-ever-afters and the most gorgeous heroes you can imagine. These handsome, caring men definitely have forever in mind!

July also continues our WRITTEN IN THE STARS series. Each month in 1992, we're proud to present a book that focuses on the hero and his astrological sign. This month we're featuring the passionate, protective Cancer man in Diana Whitney's utterly charming *The Last Bachelor*.

In months to come, watch for Silhouette Romance novels by your all-time favorites, including Diana Palmer, Suzanne Carey, Annette Broadrick and Brittany Young.

The Silhouette Romance authors and editors love to hear from readers, and we'd love to hear from *you*.

Until next month . . . happy reading!

Valerie Susan Hayward
Senior Editor

DIANA WHITNEY

The Last Bachelor

Silhouette Romance

Published by Silhouette Books New York

America's Publisher of Contemporary Romance

To Rob and Lana, good friends who have taught us
the joys and pitfalls of country life.
Thanks for putting up with us!

SILHOUETTE BOOKS
300 E. 42nd St., New York, N.Y. 10017

THE LAST BACHELOR

Copyright © 1992 by Diana Hinz

ISBN: 0-373-08874-4

First Silhouette Books printing July 1992

Printed in the U.S.A.

DIANA WHITNEY

The moody Cancerian man, the intuitive Pisces woman—I love these people. I understand them because my own sign, Scorpio, completes the watery trio.

Water people are a mysterious lot, secretive and universally misunderstood by those born under earthier planetary influences. As a group, we are an enigma to the logical Aquarian, a perplexing oddity to the staid Taurus and an irresistible challenge to the fiery Aries. No one truly understands us. We like it that way.

Ask my Libra husband, poor dear. As he balances his way through life, questioning every aspect of the most minute decision, I pass swift and instinctive judgment on matters large or small. He stoically accepts my peculiarities. I try not to gloat when I'm right. Astrologically, we may seem incompatible, but for those who cherish romance, there is but one truth in the cosmic heart. To us, true love has always been WRITTEN IN THE STARS.

CANCER

Fourth sign of the Zodiac
June 21 to July 22
Symbol: Crab
Planet: Moon
Element: Water
Stone: Pearl
Color: Pale blue
Metal: Silver
Flower: Larkspur
Lucky Day: Monday
Countries: Scotland, United States, West Africa
Cities: New York, Stockholm, Venice

Famous Cancers

Bill Cosby
Robin Williams
Harrison Ford
Nelson Rockefeller

Nancy Reagan
Ann Landers
Princess Diana
Lena Horne

★

Chapter One

Lenore Gregory Blaine rushed through the lobby of the Golden Years retirement complex and hurried down the carpeted corridor toward the recreation room. She glanced anxiously at her watch and frowned.

She probably should have called first. Grandma Hettie wasn't one to spend an evening twiddling her thumbs waiting for a dinner invitation. In fact, Hester Elizabeth Gregory rarely waited for anything. The peppery woman propelled herself like a silver-headed missile, unwilling to miss a single delicious experience that life had to offer.

Lenore frequently found her grandmother's warp-speed life-style exhausting but after a particularly grueling day, she longed to bask in the older woman's exuberant glow and for a few brief hours, to free her troubled mind. As grueling days went, this one had been a real bummer.

When Lenore reached the mauve and paisley rec room, she stepped quietly inside. The intimate area was warm and inviting, scented by lemon wax and usually humming with activity. Tonight, however, the group of residents lounging around the huge television seemed unusually quiet. In a moment, Lenore realized why.

Her grandmother wasn't here. Lenore's heart sank. No wonder the atmosphere was so dismal. Normally Hettie would be transforming the daily news into a lively debate on society's social and political ills. Such discussions normally vacillated from boisterous to outrageous and Hettie enjoyed them immensely, taking great pride in popping the pompous egos of blatantly conservative peers.

But tonight there was no discussion, no debate, only the droning voice of the newscaster to drown out the bored sighs of the audience.

Apparently Hettie had made other plans for the evening. That wasn't particularly unusual but Lenore was deeply disappointed.

A masculine voice jolted her. "Miss Gregory?"

Lenore turned and stared into a pair of startling green, vaguely familiar eyes. "Blaine," she corrected. "Gregory is my maiden name."

"Yes, of course," the man mumbled absently, dismissing the information with a nonchalant wave. Then he proceeded to unzip his aviator jacket and ignored Lenore while he scrutinized the room.

"Is there something I can do for you?" Lenore inquired politely.

"Yes, thank you." He pursed his lips, continuing to stare over her head.

Patiently she awaited further details, but he seemed to have forgotten that she was even there. Ordinarily Lenore would have shrugged and walked off, but she was oddly compelled to stay. Just for a few minutes, of course, to see what this peculiar guy was up to.

Although he carried himself with great authority, his eyes betrayed a subtle anxiety that was fascinating. Most people would have been intimidated by his imperious manner but Lenore was simply amused. It was enjoyably ludicrous to see a man dressed in black leather and faded blue jeans conducting himself like European royalty.

Actually the guy didn't come across as particularly arrogant, just a bit distracted. Lenore could certainly relate to that.

Besides with that mass of black hair and dark chiseled features, his aloofness simply added to the delicious mystery. It also tweaked her playful spirit.

"You know, I ask myself why a man with a jacket full of zippers and a worn T-shirt would be haunting the halls of a retirement complex," she mused aloud. "Let's see, there's no pizza box under your arm and you certainly don't look like an insurance salesman. I mean, I'm sure there's nothing kinky going on but some of these old gals are pretty spry—"

That got his attention. *"Kinky?"* He was obviously appalled and bewildered. "I...beg your pardon?"

When he looked straight at her, those clear green eyes seemed to generate their own light. Lenore took an involuntary step backward. She remembered those eyes. More precisely, she remembered the effect they had on her. She just couldn't put her finger on exactly where or when.

While she racked her memory, he offered a clue. "I'm looking for my uncle."

"Your uncle?"

He pinned her with a stare so intense that Lenore nearly forgot to breathe. "Yes, my uncle," he replied impatiently. "Edison Collier."

Lenore snapped her fingers in recognition. "I remember now. We met at the complex bridge tournament a couple of months ago. You're Sonny's nephew...uh...Sheldon?"

The man winced. "Steven. Steven Collier."

"Oh, sorry. Anyway, Grandma told me that your uncle is the best bridge partner she ever had. Just rotten luck that they didn't take the championship. Personally I think there was some illegal signals going on, don't you? I mean, when Mrs. Rienhold sneezed and her teeth fell on the table right before her partner bid four no-trump, well, you've got to admit that the timing was just a bit too convenient."

Steven blinked in astonishment. "I...must have missed that."

"Too bad. It was quite exciting."

"I can imagine." Steven shifted uncomfortably and seemed bewildered, as though losing control of a conversation was completely alien to him.

It probably was. At the bridge tournament, Steven Collier had watched Lenore with an acute intensity that she'd found both intriguing and chilling. When they'd been introduced, his palm had closed around hers with a gentle firmness that lingered a bit too long. His touch had conveyed interest, yet he'd scowled constantly and his eyes had been tinged with suspicion.

Now Lenore observed him more closely. He was obviously ill at ease yet his sharp features were as cool and distant as a lunar landscape. But even the dark side of the moon hid a luminous warmth lurking just beyond the shadows. Lenore had felt that warmth then. She still did.

Then Lenore noted a faint flicker of uncertainty in those crystal-green eyes and intuitively felt the heat radiating from beneath the hardened surface. The shell cracked and Lenore could peek inside. In that unguarded moment she glimpsed an unanticipated sensitivity that was curiously unnerving.

Rattled, Lenore avoided Steven's gaze and fiddled with her purse strap and strained for a casual, unaffected comment. "Actually your uncle is a charming man. He has a quirky sense of humor, but then so does my grandmother. That's probably why they get along so well."

Steven raked his fingers through the mass of thick black hair and cleared his throat. "As a matter of fact, that's exactly what I wanted to discuss with you."

"Your uncle's sense of humor?"

"No, of course not." His impatient frown returned. "Edison and your grandmother have been spending a great deal of time together."

Lenore cocked her head. "Grandma has a lot of friends."

"I'm sure she does. She's a very, uh, unique woman."

That was certainly an understatement. Lenore made no attempt to hide her amusement but her tickled grin seemed to cause Steven even more discomfort, so she simply said, "I've always thought so."

He nodded morosely and jammed his hands into his pockets. "I haven't been able to reach my uncle this afternoon."

Lenore instantly sobered. "Do you think he might be ill? The complex manager has a master key—"

"I'm certain he's fine," Steven said quickly, then added under his breath, "Physically, at least." Before she questioned that bizarre statement, he added, "I just thought you might be able to help me."

Now Lenore was bewildered. "How could I possibly help?"

"Because of Edison's friendship with Mrs. Gregory—"

Lenore interrupted. "Hettie."

"Excuse me?"

"Everyone calls Grandma Hettie. She hates formality."

Steven mumbled something unintelligible and took a deep breath. "Do you know if my uncle and your grandmother are together?"

His tone indicated that he was definitely not pleased by the prospect but before Lenore could respond, an excited buzz emanated from the gathering by the television. Automatically Steven and Lenore both glanced toward the group where several residents were wagging eager fingers at the set. For a moment, Lenore couldn't figure out what all the fuss was about. After all, news coverage of political demonstrations was pretty routine stuff.

As Lenore studied the screen, she heard Steven's outraged gasp just as a familiar silvery head caught her eye. There, in big screen living color, were Hettie and Edison, protest signs in hand, being escorted to a paddy wagon by local police.

The color drained from Steven's face and Lenore feared he was going into shock. He blinked rapidly, as though the frantic movement could erase what he'd just seen.

Lenore smiled tolerantly and glanced at her watch. "We'd better get going. The Valley Precinct cashier closes up at 7:00 p.m. and if we don't pay the fine by then, they'll have to spend the night there."

Steven emitted a sick, gurgling sound. "In . . . jail?"

"Hmm." Lenore pulled a thick ring of car keys from her purse. "Do you know how to get there?"

The man looked positively ill. His mouth opened but no sound emerged. Lenore realized that the poor man was truly distressed and felt a surge of sympathy.

"It's only a misdemeanor citation," she said gently.

Steven stared in disbelief. "You've been through this before."

Lenore shrugged. "A few times. Grandma's always lobbying for something. It's really no big deal."

Although Lenore had meant to calm him, her comment seemed to have the opposite effect. Steven's expression flickered from merely appalled to absolutely horrified. She sighed. It was going to be a long night.

But an interesting one.

For Steven, the entire ordeal had been nothing less than a nightmare. He simply couldn't believe his uncle had actually allowed himself to become involved in such a distasteful situation.

In his prime, Edison Collier had been powerful and brilliant, scrupulous about obeying rules. In fact, he may have been the only man in America who'd never cheated on his income tax. At seventy-eight, Edison had never even had so much as a parking ticket.

So how could this have happened? Why would a man who'd walked six blocks out of his way rather than jaywalk suddenly commit a willful trespass and allow himself to be hauled off to jail? The answer seemed painfully clear.

Hester Gregory.

When Edison had inexplicably chosen the Golden Years complex, Steven had been apprehensive, believing that his uncle could do better than a crowded retirement complex catering to social security recipients. Apparently, his concern had been well placed. Through this hellish turn of events, it had become increasingly apparent that the ditsy old woman and her motor-mouthed granddaughter had more than a passing acquaintance with the inside of a police station. In fact, the desk sergeant had greeted Lenore enthusiastically and the two of them were still chatting like chums.

Ignored, Steven had been cooling his heels and growing angrier by the minute. Finally he stomped over to the desk. "At the risk of interrupting this cozy conversation, would someone mind telling me exactly where my uncle is? If it wouldn't be too damn much trouble, that is."

The sergeant eyed him suspiciously. "Who the hell are you?"

Steven was in no mood to be cautious and apparently Lenore recognized that his response might not be particularly respectful. She snagged his arm and offered a joking remark to the scowling sergeant, then managed to haul Steven across the room. When they were safely out of earshot, she whirled on him.

"You're not too bright, are you?" she whispered fiercely. "I thought you wanted Edison out, but if you'd rather share his austere accommodations, one more wisecrack ought to do it."

"Oh, well, excuse me, but not everyone has your extensive experience in the fine art of finessing a cop."

"Common sense and good manners are not a crime, Mr. Collier. Now get that chip off your shoulder and screw those bulging eyeballs back into your head before the sergeant decides to hustle you off for observation."

With that pronouncement, Lenore took Steven's arm and favored the brooding desk officer with a dazzling smile. As she did so, she spoke without moving her lips. "Try to look pleasant."

Steven glared at her. "I want to see my uncle."

With a resigned sigh, Lenore let go of his arm. "They're releasing him now. Good grief, you act as though Edison is a wayward teenager instead of a grown man who has survived nearly eight decades. Don't you think you're being just a tad overprotective?"

The astute observation was sobering. Steven rubbed his face and turned away. Up to a point, she was right. He *was* protective of his uncle, but he had good reason to be. Experience had taught Steven that wisdom wasn't an automatic gift of age. Elderly people often trusted too easily and when that trust was betrayed, the result was always tragic—and sometimes fatal.

Steven couldn't forget the helpless horror of having seen other lives destroyed by greed and deceit. He was determined that his uncle would not suffer the same unfortunate fate. Those who believed Edison Collier to be a profitable victim would have to deal with Steven first. Then, God help them.

Lenore interrupted his chilling thoughts with a breathless exclamation. "Here they come! See, I told you they wouldn't be shipped off for dog food. Edison! Over here!"

From the desk, Edison waved happily, then turned his attention to signing some kind of papers. When he finished, he strode briskly across the lobby.

Steven was relieved to note that his uncle looked none the worse for wear. In fact, the old codger was actually smiling. That wouldn't ordinarily be unusual, but Edison had always been a particularly somber individual who viewed life as a serious business and frivolity as useless escapism. Now, after having been booked and fingerprinted and hauled off to the hootskow, Steven's staid uncle was grinning like a five-year-old on Christmas morning. It was all too strange.

Steven stepped forward anxiously. "Are you all right?"

Thick lenses magnified Edison's delighted blue eyes. "Steven! I didn't expect to see you here."

"That makes us even," Steven replied dryly.

At that moment, the scent of sweet lilac wafted into the lobby and Steven glimpsed a bouncing mop of silvery curls as Hester Gregory swept in like a silver-topped tornado. She was talking a blue streak and the incoherent words, punctuated by brief spurts of tinkling laughter, rushed past Steven's stunned ears like a swarm of happy insects.

Hettie was just as Steven remembered, a munchkin of a woman who balanced a ballooning figure on shapely calves and tiny feet that hinted at the svelteness of youth. She must have once been beautiful and in fact, still was, although her round little face, button nose and ball-shaped body would have seemed more appropriate on an animated snowman.

In spite of the woman's awkward shape, she moved with surprising agility as she dashed across the room to embrace Lenore. "You didn't have to come, child."

Stepping back, Lenore took her grandmother's plump hands and laughed. "I was in the neighborhood."

Hettie chuckled. "Just as well. Sonny can't play poker worth a ring-tailed hoot. Every time he drew a decent hand, his mustache twitched and everyone folded."

Edison's white head bobbed in agreement and he grinned happily. "We owe the guards seventy-five dollars."

"What?" Steven couldn't believe what he was hearing. "You were playing poker? For money?" It was inconceivable that a man who'd preached that gambling was for the indolent and idiotic could have spent the evening doing just that.

Edison nodded happily. "Hettie says I've got potential."

Hettie says.

Steven closed his eyes and tried to stay calm. It wasn't easy. Ever since Edison had hooked up with Hester Gregory, he'd turned into someone Steven hardly recognized.

Over the years Edison had repeatedly warned Steven about the peculiar effect feminine wiles had on otherwise sane and intelligent men. Edison had lived as he'd counseled, remaining a confirmed bachelor for nearly eight decades. Now Steven wondered if his uncle had forgotten the wisdom of his own dire warnings.

Steven pondered the old woman's involvement with Edison and fretted about her motives. Steven wasn't exactly paranoid but his caution had been repeatedly justified. There was something odd about the relationship between his uncle and Hester Gregory, something that went beyond casual friendship. He couldn't define his concerns but he couldn't dismiss them, either.

Edison slapped Steven's shoulder hardily, then rocked back on his heels and grinned smugly. "Did you see me on television?"

For a moment, Steven could only stare. Was he kidding? Half of Southern California had no doubt watched his elderly uncle being handcuffed and hauled away. Steven had been terrified for his uncle's safety and now everyone was standing around, grinning stupidly, as though facing off with a dozen armed policemen was actually great sport. The tension of the past hours sharpened his response. "Do you realize how dangerous that stunt was?"

Edison's smile faded. "Dangerous?"

"Yes, dangerous." Steven clenched his teeth and spoke in clipped tones. "What if a riot had broken out? You could have been seriously injured. What in the world did you think you were doing out there?"

Edison blinked. "Doing? Why, exercising my constitutional right. Did you know that those fools at city hall plan to close down the senior citizen center and reduce the school lunch budget by over forty percent? And then the incompetent boobs voted themselves a pay raise. That's unconscionable."

As Edison spoke, Hettie smiled up with obvious affection and nodded in vigorous agreement.

For a moment, Steven was speechless. At one time Edison had known everyone in city hall, from elected officials to clerk typists on a first-name basis. He'd always claimed that special treatment yielded special results and a greased rail gave a smoother ride. This sudden embrace of politically radical views was unnerving to say the least and Steven had no doubt as to who was responsible for his uncle's bizarre about-face.

Steven eyed Hettie skeptically and wondered what else she had in mind. Sabotaging a nuclear plant? Sinking a whaler? Or maybe she was some kind of cult guru, picking gullible pockets by preaching the evils of material wealth.

Rubbing his forehead, Steven suppressed such unpleasant speculation and addressed his uncle in a reasonable, although somewhat forced tone. "Couldn't you have simply expressed your views in a letter?"

With a disgusted snort, Edison waved away the suggestion with a flick of a bony hand. "Damned fools probably can't read. Besides, Hettie says that nothing gets a politician's attention like a thirty-second spot on the five o'clock news."

Hettie says.

Reasonable flew out the window. Steven's blood pressure soared along with his voice. "So you decided to get yourself arrested in front of a dozen television cameras?"

Before Edison could reply, Hettie bounced forward one step. "Oh, that was just a little misunderstanding."

Steven stared into the older woman's bright little eyes and his righteous anger instantly melted.

Sensing her advantage, Hettie rattled on before Steven could so much as open his mouth. She took his arm, patted his hand and launched into an exuberant explanation. "Now, we knew the mayor would be none too pleased by such shenanigans outside his big impressive office, so we planned a quick live feed to the studio, then we'd pack up our signs and be gone before he could do anything but cuss... did you know that the police chief is the mayor's brother-in-law?"

"Well, no..."

"Yes, indeed." Hettie's head bobbed until her gray curls vibrated. "The mayor appointed the chief not a month after the wedding. Anyway, the camera crews were late setting up so we ended up marching up and down that stupid sidewalk for nearly half an hour." She laughed delightedly. "So you see, it was all a matter of timing. When were you born?"

"Excuse me?"

"Your birthday," Hettie replied patiently. "What month were you born?"

"Ah... July, but—"

"Oh, well, that explains it." Without releasing Steven's arm, Hettie turned toward Edison and Lenore. "Cancer men are always crabby during a waning moon. In a few days he'll perk up and be back to his sensitive, charming self, won't you, dear?"

The last few words were directed toward Steven, who was astonished by the older woman's appraisal and bewildered that he didn't feel insulted by her blunt observation. He glanced helplessly toward Lenore, who was watching the entire scene with obvious amusement. The single dimple in her left cheek deepened and Steven wondered why he hadn't noticed before that her lips were exceedingly full and lush.

Hettie's nonstop banter continued. "...Lenore is a Pisces—water signs are quite compatible, you know..."

He was vaguely aware of Hettie's rapid-fire chatter but was suddenly too distracted by Lenore's mouth to pay much attention to what was being said.

"...Except for Scorpios. My late husband was a Scorpio, God love him. Never a dull moment with that man. Passionate, he was, and excitable?" The older woman chuckled and made a low whistling sound. "Gracious me! Why I remember..."

Hettie's voice became a pleasant buzz as Steven scrutinized Lenore more closely. He wasn't interested in a romantic sense, of course, but was curious as to what else he might have missed.

Individually taken, her features were quite average—a sturdy little nose and unimpressive brown hair bluntly cut at chin length. Still, she was taller than he'd realized, probably five-eight or better, and her willowy figure didn't quite match the rounded contours of her face. She bore little resemblance to her grandmother, except for the eyes. They weren't blue or brown or green, but a multihued combination that defied description.

When their eyes met, Lenore grinned openly and shrugged her eyebrows slightly as though conveying that as far as her grandmother was concerned, Steven was on his own.

So as Hettie hung on to his arm and assaulted his senses with an energetic monologue, Steven did what any red-blooded Cancerian male would do when faced with a spiraling loss of control. He folded his arms, frowned and retreated into his shell.

Lenore had watched Steven's confusion with sympathy and understanding. The man's peevishness was a bit annoying, but his concern for his uncle had been genuine. Lenore could certainly appreciate that. She felt the same about her beloved grandmother and was frequently frightened by

Hettie's unpredictable and occasionally dangerous escapades.

Lenore had learned to cope out of necessity. Coping, however, didn't seem to be Steven's strong suit. His protectiveness was about as subtle as a suit of neon armor.

Although Lenore worked hard to convey a fancy-free attitude, her own worries were tucked quietly away. At night, those fears escaped, fleeing into her dreams and mingling with terrors of the past. Awakened by her own soundless screams, she'd cower in the darkness, unable to distinguish between remembered horrors and the surrealistic rumblings of her sleeping mind.

From across the police station lobby, a peal of familiar laughter interrupted Lenore's somber thoughts and her heart swelled with love. Ever since she'd been a toddler, Lenore had openly adored her grandmother. There was no hurt so large that Hettie couldn't make better with a kiss or a smile.

No hurt but one.

Lenore shook off the memory as Hettie tottled over and snagged her arm. As they walked toward the parking lot, Hettie bobbed her head toward Steven, who was seriously engrossed in conversation with his uncle. "What do you think?" she whispered, then continued without giving Lenore a chance to respond. "Such a nice young man. Steven has never been married, you know."

Lenore couldn't fathom why her grandmother thought that information relevant but Hettie was on a roll, so Lenore made no attempt to speak.

"He's smart, too. Why, after he took over Sonny's construction firm, business increased twenty percent. Isn't that something?" Hettie paused, allowing Lenore to nod briefly. "And he's only thirty-six. He has a bright future, too. Why, one of those slick city magazines actually wrote that he was one of L.A.'s most eligible bachelors. Isn't that a kick? He's almost a celebrity!"

Lenore took advantage of Hettie's need to breathe. "Why are you telling me all this, Grandma?"

"Just thought you might be interested," Hettie replied innocently. "You've got to admit, he's a mighty foxy dude."

"Foxy dude? Have you been watching MTV again?" Lenore laughed and shook her head. Hettie was full of surprises. That was one of the reasons Lenore loved to be with her, but a point-by-point rundown of Steven Collier's virtues was wasted on Lenore, and Hettie of all people should certainly realize that.

Of course, the man did exude a certain charisma. There was a subtle defiance in his gaze that hinted of a rebel soul lurking below the tightly controlled surface. For a woman excited by challenge, Steven Collier was undeniably attractive.

Lenore simply wasn't in the market for excitement or challenge. At twenty-nine, she'd acquired an immunity to the masculine mystique and was grateful for it. She'd been in love once. Once had been enough.

Lenore glanced up and realized that they had left the building. Outside, the night air was spring cool and just slightly crisp. A few stars were visible, having fought off the city's reflecting light. As they reached the parking lot, Lenore was aware of an increased tension in the conversation between Steven and his uncle.

Although she only caught part of what Steven was saying, his disappointment was apparent. "...A season ticket at field level on the first base line." As Steven spoke, he laid a coaxing hand on his uncle's shoulder. "It was just blind luck that I was around when the box owner was called out of town."

Edison shook his head sadly. "I'd sure like to go with you, but there's this rally down at the senior center."

Steven's hand fell away and he straightened. "What kind of rally?"

"A postprotest rally. Hettie's one of the main speakers," Edison added proudly. "She's real good at a microphone."

"I'll bet," Steven mumbled, then jammed his hands into his pockets.

Steven's forlorn expression touched Lenore and she suspected that he was hurt by the perceived rejection. Apparently Edison, too, was affected. He shifted uncomfortably and glanced at his watch. "I might be able to get away early and meet you there. We could watch the last few innings together.''

Steven shook his head and managed a smile. ''No, you go ahead with your plans. There will be other games.''

''Well, if you really don't mind...''

''Not at all,'' he said firmly and almost convincingly, then tossed a reassuring arm around his uncle's thin shoulders. ''Have a good time.''

Edison beamed.

If Lenore had any doubts about how deeply Steven cared for his sweet old uncle, the tender scene she'd just witnessed had eliminated them.

Hettie's eyes took on a shrewd glow and to Lenore's horror, she planted herself directly in front of Steven. ''Lenore *loves* baseball. She was the best pitcher Solomon Junior High ever had...three no-hitters...or was it four? Never mind. Anyway there's simply no reason to let those lovely seats go empty, is there?''

Ignoring Steven's crestfallen expression, Hettie tugged on the startled man until he was standing beside Lenore. Obviously pleased with herself, she smiled brightly and rubbed her hands together. ''You two run along now. Have fun.''

Before either Lenore or Steven could so much as open their mouths, Hettie and Edison had disappeared into the darkness.

Finally Lenore managed a nervous laugh and pushed a loose strand of hair behind one ear. ''Sorry about that.''

''Ah...no problem.'' He angled a wary glance. ''You don't really like baseball, do you?''

Something about his apprehensive expression brought out the mischief in her. She smiled sweetly. ''I adore it.''

''*Ball three?* Are you crazy?'' Lenore stood, hands cupping her mouth to assure that the offending umpire could hear her displeasure. ''If that pitch had been any sweeter it'd be fattening.''

From the row in front of them, a man wearing a blue Dodger cap turned in his seat and gave Lenore a withering look. Quickly Steven grabbed her elbow and pulled her unceremoniously back into her seat. "If you're going to make a spectacle of yourself, can't you at least cheer for the home team?"

"Cincinnati is the best team in the league," she replied breathlessly. "If their starting lineup stays healthy, the Reds are a cinch to make the pennant. The Dodgers are running on empty. Their only decent catcher has rusty knees and the bull pen is so wild, they couldn't hold a ten-run lead in the bottom of the ninth."

The blue-hatted fan glared over his shoulder. At that moment, a sharp crack emanated from the field and the spectators issued a collective roar of approval quickly followed by a disappointed moan as the player was thrown out.

Instantly Lenore was on her feet, cheering Cincinnati's outfield prowess. "*Yes!* Good arm, Jackson. Way to go-o-o-o!"

Steven cringed as a dozen eyes turned in their direction. The attention Lenore's exuberance drew was disquieting and he fervently wished that he'd used the damned tickets for compost instead of allowing himself to be rooked into this humiliating ordeal.

When the Reds finally came to bat, things got even worse. Out of fifty thousand spectators in the huge coliseum, Steven heard only Lenore's voice raised in support of the visiting team.

Hoping to make himself less visible, Steven tried to slide down in his seat but was startled by Lenore's sudden gasp. He straightened quickly. "What's wrong?"

"Look!" She wiggled her finger frantically. "There, in the on-deck circle. It's Dan-The-Man."

"Who?" Steven squinted at the appointed area and saw a pink-cheeked Cincinnati player testing a weighted bat.

Ignoring the question, Lenore jumped to her feet and waved. "Hey, Danny! Welcome back."

Because they were seated so close to the field, Dan-The-Man actually heard Lenore's jubilant cry and glanced around, appearing surprised to be so warmly greeted on the opposition's home turf. When he spotted Lenore, who was whistling and gesturing wildly, he tipped his cap in her direction.

Lenore pointed toward the outfield and called out. "Show 'em what you can do." The young man grinned and nodded as Lenore plopped back into her seat.

Beside her, a boy of perhaps ten had been watching the exchange with great interest. "Gee," the youngster said, obviously impressed. "Do you know a real ball player?"

"I know about him," Lenore replied. "He batted three-eighteen in his rookie year *and* won a Golden Glove. Then last spring he hurt his leg and was out for the entire season. The doctors said that he'd never play again."

Several spectators were listening to the exchange and a man that Steven assumed to be the boy's father leaned forward. "Looks like the doctors were wrong."

Lenore laughed, a soft, husky sound that caused a peculiar tingling in Steven's spine. "They didn't realize how courageous and determined he was," she explained. "Dan showed up at spring training and told the manager that if they gave him a chance, he'd make it worth their while. In fact, he promised to play without a contract and if he wasn't hitting over three hundred by July first, he'd finish the season with no pay. Somehow he even got the players' union to go along with the deal."

The youngster's eyes widened. "Wow."

"So how's he doing so far this season?" the man asked.

"This is his first game," Lenore told him. "You can imagine how nervous the poor guy must be."

"Then we should be real nice to him." This suggestion came from the boy, who promptly stood up and yelled, "Hit a homer, Dan!"

The annoyed fan in front turned again, as did his two beer-drinking and exceedingly large buddies. Only Steven seemed to notice that all three men were glaring with a venom that went beyond mere irritation.

Then Dan-The-Man started walking toward the batter's box and Steven suddenly realized that Lenore, the boy and his father, and several other nearby spectators were on their feet. With Lenore as their cheerleader, the group began to holler in unison: "Go, Danny, go!" *Clap, clap.* "Go, Danny, go!"

Steven covered his eyes and slumped down. He could feel the heat from the burly group in front of them and could only hope that they hadn't consumed as much beer as the wafting odor would indicate.

Maybe Dan-The-Man would strike out.

Crack.

Steven moaned as Lenore's group screamed their approval. When two Cincinnati runs scored, it was all too much for the home-team fans. The largest and furriest of the group lurched drunkenly to his feet. "Why don' you jus' shut the hell up, lady."

Surprised, Lenore looked at the swaying man. "Are you speaking to me?"

The man belched. "Lasorda's boys are gonna stomp them stinkin' Reds into pink pulp."

Lenore smiled sweetly. "I sincerely doubt that."

The other two men stood, chests puffed and lips twisted angrily. The blue-hatted one reached out and grabbed Lenore's wrist. "You callin' my frien' a liar?"

Instantly Steven was on his feet, positioning himself between Lenore and the drunken fan. He clamped the man's forearm in a viselike grip and spoke through clenched teeth. "Let go of the lady."

Blue Hat sneered. "Who's gonna make me?"

The sight of that cruel, hairy hand bruising Lenore's fragile wrist was more than Steven could stand. He felt the cold fury surge from his very core. Twisting his grip, he dug one finger into the sensitive pressure point just behind the guy's wrist bone. The maneuver worked nicely. Blue Hat howled in pain and instantly released Lenore, who fell awkwardly backward. Quickly Steven dropped the man's hand and steadied Lenore. As she looked over Steven's shoulder, her eyes widened and he turned to follow her gaze.

Then his world exploded.

Chapter Two

Waiting impatiently outside the hospital emergency room door, Lenore glanced at her watch and realized that Steven had been wheeled off to X ray nearly thirty minutes ago. She nervously chewed her lip and wondered if his injuries had been more serious than she'd first believed.

After the brief scuffle at the ball game, Lenore had managed to drag Steven away before the incident escalated into a full-scale riot. That hadn't been easy. Being sucker-punched by a drunken Neanderthal had done little to soften Steven's dour mood. He'd risen from the concrete steps in a white-hot fury, fists clenched and eyes spitting green fire.

Ignoring the three-to-one odds, Steven would have lunged into the midst of the beefy bunch had Lenore not hauled him away. He'd resisted, of course, but having been somewhat dazed by the ferocious blow, he'd finally given in to Lenore's persistent tugging.

Once the full impact of pain hit, Steven had willingly handed Lenore the keys to his truck, dropped his head into his hands and moaned all the way to the hospital. By the time they'd arrived, he had been spitting blood and Lenore had been worried.

Now she folded her arms and fought a new surge of fear. Once Lenore had been blissfully naive of how fragile life could be. She'd believed that tragedy touched only faceless strangers and was an occurrence rare enough to rate headlines in the morning news. Mortality had been a rather vague concept shadowing a future too distant to warrant immediate concern. Then reality had struck a swift, merciless blow and Lenore's happy illusions had been shattered.

Death had become personal.

The sterile hospital waiting room suddenly seemed stifling. She wanted out. Now.

Intellectually, Lenore realized that there was no place to hide from the past but her chest still constricted and her heart raced wildly.

As she fought the overwhelming urge to run, a familiar and thoroughly perturbed voice filtered into the hallway. "I don't need a damn wheelchair."

"Hospital policy," came the cheerful feminine reply. The door burst open and Steven, bruised and sullen, was wheeled into the hallway by a smiling nurse. "There we go, good as new."

Steven growled and folded his arms. The left side of his jaw was swollen and had darkened to an ugly shade of purple, and a white bandage covered the cut on his brow. A sympathetic lump lodged in Lenore's throat as she remembered the sickening thud of his forehead slamming the concrete stadium steps.

She leaned over and patted his hand. "How are you feeling?"

He glared up. "Just ducky," he snapped, then winced and gingerly touched his puffy upper lip.

"He should see a dentist about that broken tooth as soon as possible," the nurse told Lenore, apparently assuming her to be Steven's personal caretaker. "Although the X rays showed no fractures, the stitches inside his mouth will be sore for a few days. This prescription should help. Give him one tablet every four hours as needed and have him follow up with his regular physician in about seven days."

The nurse gave the medication to Lenore. Steven immediately reached up and plucked the bottle from Lenore's outstretched palm. "I can take my own pills," he muttered peevishly. "And I don't appreciate being discussed like I'm not even here."

With a delighted laugh, the nurse ruffled Steven's hair as though he were a five-year-old. "My, aren't we grumpy tonight?"

Steven's eyes narrowed. He leaped from the chair and stomped down the corridor in an obvious fit of pique.

As Lenore followed, she smiled over her shoulder. "He can't help himself," she told the nurse. "It's the waning moon."

Lenore finally caught up with Steven in the parking lot. He stood like a brooding statue, glaring into the darkness. "I don't remember where the truck is parked," he said glumly.

"I'm not surprised. You didn't seem particularly observant when we arrived." Lenore's voice softened and she touched his shoulder. "Are you in much pain?"

Her sympathetic inquiry seemed to startle him, as did her delicate touch. She felt his muscles quiver slightly, then he tensed as though steeling himself.

Finally he shrugged. "It only hurts when I laugh."

Lenore smiled. "Can you? Laugh, that is."

He gave her a hard stare. "This hasn't been a particularly amusing day, thanks to you and your grandmother."

"You think this is all our fault?"

"Of course, it is. None of this would have happened if the women in your family didn't have such a penchant for courting disaster. What really irks me is how you can just saunter away unscathed and oblivious to the chaos left in your wake."

"Ouch." She pulled an imaginary knife from her heart. "Actually the women in my family are known for their loyalty and dedication."

"Dedication to what? Anarchy?"

"Now don't be testy. You shouldn't have gotten involved in a brawl in the first place."

Steven's eyes widened and he shook his head in disbelief. "The drunken louse actually *grabbed* you. What was I supposed to do, pretend you were shaking hands with him?"

"I could have dealt with it."

"How, by chattering at him until he lost consciousness?"

Lenore chuckled. She knew Steven's comment was meant as a sarcastic jab but it was nonetheless a fairly accurate assessment. Since Lenore shared her grandmother's gift of gab, she was certain that she could have diffused the incident without bloodshed. To Lenore, the entire incident had been a dangerous and unnecessary display of machismo but she kept that opinion to herself to avoid hurting Steven's feelings. After all, he'd put himself in jeopardy trying to protect her. That had been rather sweet. The least she could do was to return the courtesy by not pointing out that it had also been extremely stupid.

"I know you were just trying to be helpful and I do appreciate it," Lenore told him, then added, "You were very brave."

Steven's brows knitted into a black scowl. "Don't patronize me."

"No, I really mean it. Standing up to those men was really quite gallant."

Steven didn't feel particularly gallant. He felt like a fool. To be publicly flattened was bad enough but what really stuck in his craw was the fact that Lenore had dragged him off before he could return the favor. The satisfaction of knowing the other guy was in worse shape could have gone a long way toward easing his aching jaw.

The entire evening had been a series of disasters revolving around Lenore and her wacky grandmother. Steven wondered it there was some kind of sinister plot here. Model citizens like Uncle Edison simply didn't get arrested every day and Steven hadn't actually been involved in a fistfight since college. It was all too bizarre.

If this dimpled young woman wanted to spend her life bailing Grandma out of jail, that was her business but at the moment Steven was exhausted and frustrated, not to mention being seriously annoyed by the uninvited intrusion into his neatly ordered life.

Still, he'd never been to a livelier baseball game.

The glare of headlights reminded him that they were standing in the middle of a parking lot. Automatically he slid one arm around Lenore's slim waist and pulled her onto the median. She felt fragile in his arms and a delicate fragrance wafted from her hair. Absently he bent closer, absorbed in identifying the enticing scent. Wildflowers, he decided, wildflowers mingled with a subtle hint of freshly cut herbs. She smelled like a spring meadow, clean and inviting.

Although the car had passed, Steven continued to hold Lenore close. Her eyes widened in surprise but she didn't protest or try to move away. Only the nervous dart of her tongue hinted that she was affected by his touch. The gesture was incredibly sensuous and he wondered if she would taste as sweet as she smelled. Tightening his grip, his gaze locked on to her soft mouth.

Reality intruded in the form of a silent warning from his throbbing brain. Stunned, he straightened. Had he nearly kissed this crazy woman? That bop on the head must have affected him more than he realized.

Instantly Steven pulled his arm away, simultaneously jamming his hands into his pockets as he stepped backward. His abrupt release caused Lenore to rock slightly and he fought the urge to steady her. When she shivered, he assumed the chill wind to be the culprit rather than an involuntary reaction to his touch.

"Are you cold?"

"A little," she admitted sheepishly. "I must have left my sweater at the ballpark."

Shrugging out of his jacket, Steven ignored her protests and firmly wrapped the leather garment around her shoulders.

"My hero yet again." She smiled gratefully and Steven felt a peculiar sensation along his spine. There was something about that one stupid dimple that made him feel kind of mushy inside.

He didn't much care for the sensation.

For her part, Lenore also seemed a bit nonplussed but covered her discomfort in the manner he'd come to expect from her. She chattered like an agitated magpie.

"I parked the truck over there. By the way, did you know your clutch is slipping? Oh, well, of course, you do. You drive it everyday, don't you?" Her laugh was a little tight as she walked briskly across the dark asphalt. Steven followed, making no effort to answer her rapid-fire questions. "Anyway, I know a great mechanic if you're interested. His little boy is in my day-care class. Did you know that I run a preschool? I love it, too. The kids are super, so full of wonder at things grown-ups take for granted and for them, every day is filled with exciting new discoveries about the world. It's a real joy to see how..." Her voice trailed off and she stopped so abruptly that Steven nearly plowed into her.

"Hey!" He quickly sidestepped but his annoyance melted when he saw Lenore's pensive gaze. At that moment he heard the wail of distant sirens and saw a red glow on the horizon. "Must be a fire," he commented.

In response, Lenore shivered violently and turned away. "The truck is parked here," she said dully and handed him the keys.

Since he hadn't taken any of the medication, there was no reason he shouldn't drive. Still, he'd expected her to insist on chauffeuring him at least back to the Golden Years complex where her car was parked. Instead, she listlessly opened the door and slid into the passenger seat.

He got in beside her. "Are you all right?"

She nodded and looked away, but not before Steven saw the despair in her eyes. Her tormented expression hit him like a fist in the gut.

Not knowing what else to do, he simply flipped on the ignition and pulled out of the parking lot.

The ride back to the retirement complex was fifteen of the longest minutes in Steven's life. Lenore sat quietly, staring out the window, responding to Steven's forced conversation politely and succinctly. Her sudden change was acutely disconcerting and he hadn't a clue as to why he should care, but he did.

Lenore Gregory Blaine was definitely a royal pain in the neck, yet there was an essence about her, a sparkling joy, a love for life. Still her unexplained mood swing had thrown a monkey wrench into Steven's initial assessment. Now he saw a peculiar dichotomy, an undercurrent of clandestine sadness that signaled a woman of great emotional complexity. That was unexpected and Steven reacted warily to situations that couldn't be neatly anticipated.

Steven was totally unprepared for his reaction to Lenore and that bothered him immensely. He had no idea what had caused Lenore's pain and the fact that he was so deeply touched by it was baffling.

Steven wasn't an uncaring man but he was certainly a cautious one. Acquaintances considered him remote, but those who had earned his trust considered him a fierce and devoted friend. That trust, however, and the resulting emotional connection could only evolve over time. Yet here he sat with a lump the size of Wyoming in his throat because of a woman he'd only known for a few brief, if exciting, hours.

Nothing made sense anymore. Five minutes ago, Steven would have offered a month's salary just to figure out where her Off switch was located. Now, he'd give twice that simply to make her smile again.

There was no doubt about it. The world had gone mad and taken Steven along for the ride.

The thin crescent moon delivered scant illumination on the steep path winding toward the front door of Lenore's secluded home. The pale light was enough. Lenore had lived here for five years and had frequently navigated the rough stone walkway in total darkness. She enjoyed the quiet beauty of the canyon. It served as a continual reminder that no matter how deep one person's loss, the world and all of its wonder had survived.

She needed to know that. Nature's vibrancy purified the heart, filtering darkness until only the joyful memories re-

mained. Lenore hadn't reached that stage yet. The pain stil
lingered quietly in the deepest part of her soul. Sometimes
like tonight, she would suddenly remember it all, relive it al
and the horrible grief would return.

Once inside, Lenore flipped the wall switch and the com
pact living room was bathed in warm light. Cream-colored
walls were accentuated by rich oak woodwork and the foca
point of the room were mullioned French doors opening
into a lush garden. Plant life also flourished inside, with
shiny green and variegated leaves adorning every table and
available nitch.

Furnishings were sparse and somewhat mismatched—a
worn Queen Anne sofa flanked by cushiony, traditiona
lounge chairs—but the overall effect was homey. Adding to
the comfortable charm were dozens of photos lovingly ar
ranged throughout the room, pictures of family and friends
remembrances of happier times. Lenore cherished them, as
she cherished the warm memories they evoked.

Absently dropping her purse on the credenza, Lenore
collapsed tiredly into her favorite lounge chair and closed
her eyes. Images of Steven Collier invaded her exhausted
mind. An interesting man, she mused silently, but his tough,
don't-mess-with-me frown contradicted the esoteric vulnerability in those startling green eyes. Intuitively she knew that
he wasn't as hard as he'd like people to believe and suspected he used that remote attitude as a protective shell.

The assumption was natural for Lenore. Concealment
and emotional shelter were a way of life for her, so it stood
to reason that she could recognize that guarded behavior in
others.

Actually she and Steven had quite a bit in common. They
were both nonconformists, although Lenore exploited and
enjoyed the same rebellious streak that Steven struggled to
suppress. In fact, she imagined that he'd vehemently deny
any such radical leanings but Lenore couldn't be fooled.
Tight blue jeans and black leather were more appropriate
for a tattooed biker than the CEO of a multimillion-dollar
development firm.

If his clothing was a clue, his hair was a dead giveaway. The only concession to professional image were the tapered sides, scissored to midear length. The remainder from crown to nape flowed as wildly as the windblown mane of an untamed stallion.

And Lenore had recognized that glimmer of wildness when he'd held her in his arms. He was so...male. The heat of him had permeated every pore in her body and nearly buckled her knees. Even the memory gave her chills.

Sitting up, she rubbed her burning eyelids and tried to ignore the odd tingling in her stomach. Any interest she had in Steven Collier was strictly platonic. After all, his uncle was one of Hettie's dearest friends so in a sense, Steven could almost be considered as family.

The distorted rationale almost made her laugh out loud. What ever she felt about Steven Collier, it was certainly not familial and that in itself was highly bothersome.

Leaning back, her gaze fell on the photograph of a smiling, fair-haired man. Guilt gnawed at her. She shouldn't be thinking about Steven, or any man for that matter. There had been, and would be, only one man in her life. Only Michael.

Lenore lifted the picture, touching the glass with her fingertip as she whispered his name aloud. It had been so long and yet not long enough. Had his eyes really been that blue or had the coloring been exaggerated by the photographic process? She couldn't really remember. In fact, try as she would, there was so little Lenore could actually recall about the short time they'd had together.

Their happiness had lasted only a few short months and had ended six years ago. Still, not to recapture each moment with crystal clarity seemed a betrayal of what they had shared.

In spite of her effort, time had obscured the details of their marriage. She couldn't even recall the pet name Michael had given her. It was some kind of furry-animal endearment...kitten or bunny or something equally inane but at the time, that fond sobriquet had made her pulse hop with happiness.

Lenore squeezed her eyelids shut and shook her head. It wasn't fair that she couldn't remember. Moments that had once meant everything to her were now hazy recollections while the grief, the unendurable pain of Michael's loss was indelibly etched in her memory.

That, Lenore could never forget.

Swinging around the concrete pillar, Lenore drove through the marina parking area. The sea was calm today, its glassy green surface reflecting sparkling sunlight and malformed images of puffy clouds.

Lenore braked, slowing the gray sedan to a stop. Rifling through her purse, she extracted the crumpled sheet on which she'd hastily copied Steven's address from the telephone book.

"Ocean Avenue, P17," she mumbled aloud, then glanced up and scanned the rows of neatly tied boats. At the end of the thin ribbon of asphalt lining the dock area stood a faded sign on a peeling wooden pole. This skinny, potholed path was indeed Ocean Avenue but Lenore couldn't see anything that remotely resembled an apartment building. That was odd.

Then she noticed a stenciled sign on a nearby dock—Pier 12. Her heart sank as she realized that P17 hadn't been an apartment number. Steven must actually live on one of those bobbing, rolling, stomach-turning boats.

Oh, Lord.

Lenore automatically clutched her abdomen and seriously questioned the wisdom of this little jaunt. At nine years old, Grandma Hettie and Grandpa Fred had taken Lenore to Catalina. The trip had been meant as a special birthday treat. Unfortunately the Great White Steamship had cruised less than a mile when Lenore had become violently ill. She'd spent the entire cruise in the lavatory while Hettie fussed and clucked, insisting that since Pisces is the sign of the fish, people born in March simply didn't get seasick.

In spite of Hettie's protestations, Lenore's little tummy continued to respond in a most un-Piscean manner. That had been Lenore's first experience with boats. It had also been her last. Now she could barely look at a dinghy without feeling nauseous.

So here she sat with a flask of chicken soup and nobility in her heart wondering if Florence Nightingale would have balked at tending a floating wounded warrior. Probably not.

With a resigned sigh, Lenore gathered up the thermos and stepped from the car. She looked out at the undulating sea and paused uneasily. Maybe she should forget the whole thing. After all, this mercy mission wouldn't alleviate her responsibility for last night's fiasco. Still, she was already here. Besides, the boats were tied to docks, so they weren't really moving. Well, they were rocking a little, but that wasn't the same as moving. Was it? Oh, nuts. She was so rattled that even her thoughts made no sense.

Deciding she might as well get it over with, Lenore took a deep breath, gathered her courage and strode down the crumbling asphalt toward Pier 17.

At the appointed dock, she found the *Bohemian*, an old cabin cruiser that she judged to be no more than thirty feet, but to her the darn thing looked just like a big white steamship.

Ignoring a disconcerting queasiness, she walked briskly down the pier with her high heels resolutely thunking the splintered wood. A plank had been laid from dock to boat and Lenore gingerly forded it. She'd just grabbed the smooth metal railing when a huge black animal emerged from the cabin, snarling ferociously.

The massive rottweiler planted four saucer-size paws on the deck between Lenore and the cabin door, pleated his huge muzzle and effectively displayed every one of his sharp, gleaming incisors.

Lenore, however, was not intimidated by the sight of a mere dog, no matter its size. "Hi, pooch. Are you canine security around here?"

The animal growled threateningly and a familiar, although somewhat slurred voice called from beyond the open cabin door. "Damn it, Butch, stop bullying the sea gulls and get your stubby tail back in here."

Ignoring the command, the dog responded by taking one step toward Lenore and increasing the velocity of his warning snarl.

"Butch, huh? Not a particularly inventive name but I guess it suits you." The boat rocked slightly and Lenore, who had one foot on the plank and one foot on the worn deck, instantly jumped forward, lost her balance and stumbled into the startled dog. "Sorry, boy. Haven't got my sea legs yet," she mumbled, using the animal's strong back as a prop.

Butch swung his huge head around and stared up at the odd woman hanging on to him. He tried to growl but the sound came out more like a surprised gurgle. Then Lenore cheerfully patted the rottweiler's shiny black head, straightened and headed toward the cabin door.

"Yoo-hoo," she called, bending to peer down into the dimly lit cabin. "It's your friendly neighborhood welcome committee."

Without waiting for an invitation, Lenore descended the half-dozen steps into the boat's living quarters. To her right was a tiny dining area and a galley, small and cluttered, but obviously quite serviceable. On her left, an L-shaped seating area had been built into the cabin's faded wood walls. Toward the bow of the boat was a ragged maroon curtain separating what Lenore assumed to be the sleeping area.

Above and behind her, she heard the clickity-clack of canine toenails on the deck, then felt a shadow on her back. Lenore glanced over her shoulder and saw the rottweiler gazing down with a bewildered expression. "Okay, Butch, where's he hiding?"

Butch cocked his big head quizzically. Just then the boat tilted mildly and Lenore's stomach lurched in response. She braced herself on the dinette table and glanced around the empty cabin. "I know you're in here, Steven," she called out. "I can hear you breathing."

After a moment's pause, the maroon curtain parted. There stood Steven looking like a stunned chipmunk. "Wha' in hell—"

"Oh, you poor thing! You look like you've got a baseball in your mouth." Lenore dropped her purse and the soup flask on the table and strode over to the startled man. Before he could close his swollen mouth, Lenore had taken hold of his arm and pulled him to the nearest porthole. "Turn your face toward the light," she mumbled. "Goodness, that must be terribly painful. Have you been taking your pills? Do the stitches hurt? Open your mouth and let me see."

As she reached up to touch his face Steven grasped her wrist and turned away. "Are you crazy?"

"I don't think so," Lenore replied cheerfully, brushing her palms together when he released her wrist. "Of course, that's just my opinion. Actually I've always believe insanity more of a social term than a scientific one. Some people view reality a bit differently than the majority. There's more than one version of truth, after all, and some of history's greatest philosophers were considered mad simply because their opinions deviated from accepted norms..."

As Lenore continued the one-sided dialogue, Steven squeezed his eyes shut and shook his head as though trying to awaken from a weird dream. When he opened his eyes, Lenore was still there.

And she was still talking.

"...So you can see that the word 'crazy' has been completely misused for centuries. Now, open your mouth and let me see if the stitches are inflamed." Smiling brightly, she took a step forward.

Steven instantly stepped back, shielding himself with an outstretched palm. "Stay away from me, woman."

With a soft *tsking* sound, Lenore took her purse from the table. "Men are so predictable," she said to no one in particular. "They'll wade into bloody battle with nothing more than a slingshot and a courageous heart, then faint dead away at the sight of a hypodermic needle."

Steven's eyes widened. "Needle?"

"I rest my case." Chuckling softly, Lenore reached into her purse. "Relax, Sir Galahad. No needles, but I have got something that will make you feel much better."

Apparently interested, he lifted one dark brow and leaned forward. "I hope you have a pint of rum in there."

"Nope, even better." With a flourish, she pulled out a tiny bottle.

He was obviously disappointed. "Wha's that?"

"Teething medicine."

"You're kidding."

"I use it at the day-care center for cut lips and such. It works like a charm and is perfectly safe." She rooted through her purse and pulled out a box of cotton swabs, then advanced toward Steven, who regarded her warily. "Trust me."

His eyes narrowed. "Uh-uh."

"Afraid?"

"Of course not." He stared apprehensively at the bottle and licked his puffy lips. The inside of his cheek felt like raw hamburger but he'd rather die on the spot than let this nutty woman stick her mitts into his mouth. "I feel jus' fine."

"Ah. Well since you're trying to talk without moving your lips, you must be practicing ventriloquism. Planning a career change?"

Steven frowned and folded his arms. The woman was impossible, absolutely impossible. When Butch hesitantly started down the stairs, Steven glared at the hapless animal. "Tha's the last time I put you on guard duty."

Butch whined contritely and slunk under the table.

Lenore gave Steven a reproachful look. "Don't blame the poor dog. He was really quite ferocious, weren't you, boy?" She peeked under the table and scratched the unhappy animal's chin, then straightened and cocked her head prettily. "Now, will you cooperate?"

"No." Steven lifted his chin and mustered a menacing stare.

She shrugged. "It's up to you."

Steven regarded her skeptically. Somehow, he hadn't expected her to give up so easily. He braced himself for her next maneuver when she surprised him by turning her back and busily tidying up the galley.

"Wha' are you doing?"

"I'm not going to fix your lunch on a messy counter. Germs, you know."

"I don' wan' lunch."

She opened a cupboard and peered inside. "It hurts too much to eat, doesn't it?"

Steven wasn't about to acknowledge that. "I'm jus' not hungry."

"Of course you're hungry. You're just too stubborn to admit it." Lenore continued to search through the galley cupboards. After a moment, she chortled happily and pulled out a box of sealable plastic bags. Instantly she opened the tiny refrigerator, scooped a handful of ice cubes into the bag, closed the water-tight zip seal. When she was satisfied with her handiwork, she tossed the filled bag in Steven's direction.

The unexpected gesture startled him and he barely managed to unfold his arms and catch the damned thing before it could hit him in the chest. He stared stupidly at the ice pack.

"Hold it against your face," Lenore explained patiently. "It'll reduce the swelling and make you more comfortable. Then maybe you'll be able to enjoy your lunch."

For a moment, Steven considered refusing simply on the grounds that he didn't like being told what to do. But in truth, his entire jaw throbbed like hell so he figured it couldn't hurt to give it a try. Gingerly he touched the frigid pack to his jaw and winced. The cold shock was extremely painful but he saw the amused twinkle in Lenore's eyes and was determined to give her no further reason to ridicule him. Steeling himself, he pressed the ice against his face hard enough to make his eyes water.

Then a strange thing happened. Lenore was at his side with an expression of total concern and compassion.

"Careful," she murmured softly. She took the ice pack and wrapped it with a nearby tea towel before handing it back to him. Then, taking his hand she gently guided his movements until the covered pack barely touched his swollen face. This time Steven felt no pain at all. In fact, he didn't even notice the cold. He was, however, acutely aware of her warm hand covering his, the sweetness of her breath as she crooned soft reassurances.

Her voice was hypnotic, soothing, and before Steven realized what was happening, she had coaxed him into opening his mouth and was dabbing teething anesthetic on the painfully inflamed stitches.

"Open wider," she urged, tapping his chin gently. When he responded, she pursed her lips and concentrated and stared inside.

Steven felt like a complete imbecile. Here he was, trapped like a rat with a woman he barely knew practically sitting on his chest and peering into his mouth. Even more absurd was the fact that he was actually allowing it. She leaned closer and her now familiar sweet-fresh scent enveloped him. Her touch was delicate, so gentle that he felt his taunt muscles begin to relax.

"The stitches are probably being aggravated by the sharp edge of that broken tooth," Lenore murmured. "When are you going to the dentist?"

Since his jaw was propped open, Steven's response was a bit garbled. "Isaherooon."

Amazingly enough, Lenore simply nodded. "What time this afternoon?"

"Ee-erie."

"Not until three-thirty?" She made a series of soft clucking sounds and dipped a fresh swab into the medicine bottle. "If you had said it was an emergency, they would have squeezed you in earlier. My grandfather broke a tooth once, poor man. One minute he was happily eating a bowl of applesauce and the next he was hopping all over the living room making these pitiful little grunting sounds—turn your head a little...there, that's good—and he wouldn't let Grandma call the dentist. He said it was no big deal. Well, to make a long story short—"

Steven emitted a sarcastic snort. Fat chance of that. The woman was actually wearing out his eardrums. Then he remembered how her sad silence had affected him last night and decided that no matter how frustrating, constant chatter was preferable.

Actually he discovered that if he closed his eyes and allowed his mind to drift, her voice was pleasant, melodic and strangely comforting. The soothing sound combined with the feathery touch of gentle fingers to make him feel safe and cared for. In fact, he was groggily surprised to realize that he was actually enjoying her tender ministrations.

A cold breeze brushed his chest as she suddenly stood up. "All finished, big guy."

Feeling oddly disappointed by her distance, Steven laid one palm against his swollen jaw and realized that the pain had been significantly reduced.

"Better?" she asked.

"Yes, yes, it is."

"You sound surprised."

"I am."

"Oh, ye of little faith." She picked up her purse and brushed a loose strand of hair from her face. "I'll leave the bottle. If the pain flares up again, you can reapply it. Just follow the label instructions and don't use it more than four times a day."

"Uh . . . well, thanks—"

"Oh! I almost forgot." She patted the thermos. "Chicken soup. Cures most anything. Don't be stubborn, now. Even big boys need their nourishment. Well, I've got to run. Take care."

Then with a cheerful wave, she disappeared up the stairs and left both Steven and Butch staring at the vacant doorway.

What an odd woman, Steven mused, scratching his head. Beautiful—in an understated way—but definitely marching to her own little drummer. He rather liked that but her disgusting cheeriness could drive a sane man to drink.

He glanced morosely at the brightly colored thermos and fervently wished that it contained something stronger than chicken soup. Still, Steven was pleased by the gesture and silently admitted that he'd found her entire visit to be, well, interesting. The woman was weird, certainly, but at least she wasn't boring.

Suddenly the boat that had always been Steven's refuge seemed oppressively quiet and empty. Even Butch seemed affected. The bewildered animal paced the tiny cabin, then stopped to stare morosely at the vacant stairway. The poor fellow didn't know what had hit him and the sad part was that Steven understood and shared the dog's confusion.

Suddenly restless, Steven turned on the television. Using the remote, he absently flipped from station to station as his mind wandered. Although he was still concerned about Edison's relationship with Hester Gregory, he didn't think that Lenore was capable of clandestine conspiracy. In fact, he seriously doubted if Lenore had a deceptive bone in her lithe and lovely body.

Still, his original skepticism had been justified. Although Edison was active and virile, Steven had noted a hint of impending frailty in his uncle's thinning face that was an unpleasant reminder of old man Bergstrom. Steven had been only a child, but he could still recall how much he'd adored that crusty old fellow.

Thinking back, Steven pictured the crumbling old brownstone that had been his childhood home. His parents had been alive then, struggling in that twilight zone of economic demographics known as lower middle class.

Stevie had been unaware of his parents' financial burden. To an eight-year-old, poverty was an alien term. After all, he'd never gone hungry and although his clothing had been old, designer labels hadn't been the measure of popularity at Public School 117. So Stevie had been happy in those early days, as yet untouched by the tragedies that would shape his future and mold the man he would become.

He remembered hot summer nights when the city's foul air hung like a toxic cloud, smothering and denying the momentary respite of sleep. Stevie had slipped to the fire escape, climbing up to Samuel Bergstrom's apartment. Old Sam had been an insomniac and he'd always left the window open for Stevie's midnight visits.

One night as Stevie clamored over the sill into the dingy apartment, the old man had been hunched over a newspaper. That itself was rather strange. Old Sam rarely read anything beyond the cartoons on back of cereal boxes.

Stevie had announced himself. "Hey, Sam. What's shakin'?"

The frizzy white head had lifted and rheumy red eyes peered over the newspaper. "Come on in, boy. Sit yourself."

Stevie scrambled over the rusty radiator and sat on the ottoman beside his friend's slippered feet. "Whatcha' doin'?"

Sam's wrinkles instantly rearranged into a toothless grin. "Can you keep a secret?"

Nodding vigorously, Stevie assured Sam that he could.

The old man bent forward, ancient eyes sparkling. "I'm gonna be rich, boy, richer than that Rockerfeller guy."

Stevie's eyes widened. "Numbers or horses?"

Cackling with delight, Sam shook his head and slapped his bony knee. Then he reached under the cushion of the tattered easy chair and pulled out several crisp, official-looking documents. "These is my ticket to easy street, boy."

The papers meant nothing to Stevie. "What are they?"

"Stock certificates, son. Bought 'em for a song, I did, and look here in the newspaper." He pointed to a line of odd-looking symbols. "They's worth ten times what I done paid. Why, by next week they be worth twenty times, then twenty times that."

"How do you know?"

"The man, he told me. Hated to sell, he said, but his old mammy was sick and he had to have the cash. Took every penny I had saved, but I got me a real bargain."

"Gee. Whatcha' gonna do with all that money?"

Sam curled his arthritic fingers into a semiclaw and feigned a punch at Stevie's jaw. "First, I'm gonna buy my best friend the biggest, brightest bike in the entire city."

Stevie's eyes lit like neon. "You mean . . . me?"

"'Course I mean you. Ain't we best friends?"

"You bet," Stevie replied with fervent sincerity. "You're the best friend I ever had in my whole life."

Satisfied, Sam leaned back and stared dreamily at the stained ceiling. "Then I'm gonna live like a man again. I ain't never gonna worry about havin' enough to eat or livin in pain 'cause I can't afford no medicine. I'm gonna walk down the street with my head up and folks ain't gonna call me Old Crazy Sam no more. They'll call me *Mr.* Bergstrom, by God. I'm gonna have me some respect."

A lump caught in Stevie's throat, although he wasn't quite sure why. Rich or poor, he loved Old Crazy Sam and there was nothing in the world Stevie wouldn't do for him. Still Stevie was skeptical. Something was wrong with all of this but he couldn't exactly put his finger on the problem. "Maybe you oughta take those papers somewhere, maybe a bank or something."

Blinking, Sam glanced down at the concerned boy. "How come?"

"I dunno." Stevie shrugged, suddenly uncomfortable. "So you don't get robbed or somthin'."

After considering the suggestion, Sam nodded sagely. "Good thinkin', boy. Can't be too careful nowadays."

"Yeah," Stevie agreed halfheartedly, still perplexed by a sense of impending doom. "Well, I'd better get back. See ya."

But Sam didn't respond. He was lazily gazing at the ceiling again with gleaming eyes and a satisfied smile, so Stevie slipped out to the fire escape and returned to his room.

The next day Stevie saw Sam coming home from the bank and knew something was wrong. He ran over and tugged on the old man's sleeve, but Sam ignored him and stared vacantly into space, stooped over as though the burden of a lifetime had suddenly crashed onto his frail shoulders. Sam painfully mounted the brownstone steps and went up to his barren sixth-floor apartment.

Ten minutes later, the old man stepped onto the fire escape and jumped. The worthless stock certificates were still in his pocket.

Now, twenty-eight years later, Steven still broke out in a cold sweat remembering that day. All Sam had ever wanted was security and respect. Some heartless charlatan had robbed him of that by stealing not only his life's savings but his dignity as well. Perhaps there had been nothing an eight-year-old could have done to stop the tragedy, but that knowledge didn't alleviate Steven's guilt. He had loved Sam. Somehow, he should have protected him.

The lesson of that era had been well learned. Never again would Steven stand idly by and watch someone he loved fall into a trap of fraud and deceit.

So yes, his suspicion of Hettie and Lenore *had* been justified but the more Steven thought about them, the more certain he became that he'd probably overreacted to the entire situation. Naturally he didn't care for his uncle being involved in radical politics and he absolutely abhorred the thought of Edison being arrested, regardless of how minor the infraction. Still, the spry old woman seemed harmless enough and Lenore was the most honest and unaffected woman he'd ever met.

Something on the television screen suddenly caught Steven's attention. A program, one of those Criminal At Large shows, was profiling an elderly woman who preyed on wealthy senior citizens.

Steven leaned forward, dreading the information that he sensed would follow. The announcer intoned somberly, explaining how the gray-haired femme fatale would romance her victim until the poor guy was too smitten to think straight. Then she'd shrewdly dupe the poor sod out of his life's savings and disappear.

The scenario played on Steven's worst fears. The memory of Old Crazy Sam's death had propelled Steven to establish a long-term investment program to assure his uncle's financial security.

Over the years Steven had been obsessed with the determination that what had happened to Sam Bergstrom would never, ever happen to Edison. Anyone who had ever hurt Edison Collier, financially or emotionally, had to deal with Steven's cold fury. Most people found that prospect rather unappealing. When it came to those he loved, Steven had no qualms about using any weapon at his disposal. Edison had always accepted and appreciated Steven's protection. Until now. Until Hettie.

When the photograph of a sweet, apple-faced old woman suddenly appeared on the screen, Steven's heart sank even further. It wasn't Hester Gregory.

But dear God, it could have been.

Chapter Three

By the time Lenore returned to the day-care center, it was nearly noon. Her assistant, Maggie MacFarland, met her at the door. "Where have you been?" the woman asked in a voice more relieved than annoyed.

"My errand took a little longer than expected." Lenore tossed her purse into the cluttered room that served as an office, then glanced at her watch. "Gracious, it's nearly time to line up our hungry little vultures for lunch. Where are the kids?"

"The cook is reading them a story." Maggie wrung her hands. "I was afraid I'd have to handle lunchtime without you."

Lenore smiled at the woman's apprehension. Maggie was a childless, middle-aged divorcée with a good heart and sagging self-esteem. Although Maggie loved children desperately, she lacked direct experience in dealing with the younger set and suffered from frequent bouts of severe self-doubt. Lenore had intuitively liked Maggie and had hired her anyway. She hadn't regretted that decision. Once engrossed with the children's activities, Maggie had blossomed.

Unfortunately when she was left in charge, Maggie's shattered lack of self-esteem reemerged and the poor woman was certain that one of the kids would sever an artery or choke on a cookie or something equally traumatic.

Repairing Maggie's ego had become one of Lenore's prime directives in life, so she simply patted the woman's shoulder. "You're more than capable of supervising lunchtime," she said soothingly. "Even though you've only been with us for a few months, the children adore you and you're absolutely wonderful with them."

Maggie brightened, then caught herself and chewed her lip. "Do... you really think so?"

"Absolutely."

For a moment, Lenore was rewarded by a grateful smile that faded all too soon. "When will Jackie be back?" Maggie inquired anxiously.

Lenore sighed. Poor Maggie was going to be a tough case. "Not until next week."

"Oh, dear."

"Now we can't have Jackie sneezing and giving all the kids her flu-bug, can we?"

Maggie hesitated, seeming to weigh the consequences before mumbling, "I suppose not, but maybe we could bring someone in for a few days?"

Lenore felt a twinge of guilt. Maggie and Jackie were the center's only full-time assistants, although several part-time helpers kept the premises up to required supervision levels at all times. Still, Lenore realized the work load had increased considerably and under ordinary conditions, she would have hired extra help in a ring-tailed minute. But these simply weren't ordinary circumstances so she pasted on her cheeriest smile and tossed a reassuring arm around Maggie's thin shoulders. "No one could handle things any better than you. Now, let's feed our starving charges."

Nodding morosely, Maggie allowed Lenore to lead her toward the brightly colored dayroom, then suddenly stopped and snapped her fingers. "Gracious, I almost forgot. Mr. Liman called."

Lenore's heart lurched into her throat. "Jerry Liman, from the bank?"

"Yes, that's the one. Anyway, he said it was regarding some matter you'd discussed with him last week."

Lenore's mouth went dry. "What exactly did he say about it?"

"Let's see . . . he said something about not being able to accommodate the request. I didn't really understand what he meant."

Lenore suddenly felt as though she was back on board the *Bohemian*. Her stomach twisted and she could swear the waxed linoleum was rolling beneath her feet. To Lenore, Jerry Liman's cryptic message was painfully clear.

And it was devastating.

The job site was a madhouse of organized chaos as a dozen crews worked feverishly to meet construction deadlines. Giant girders spired from bulldozed earth in an eerie steel skeleton shrouded by clumps of construction debris. It was difficult to believe that in a few short weeks this disorder would be transformed into a gleaming high rise and parking structure, lushly landscaped and ready for tenancy.

As was his habit, Steven had spent the early hours inspecting the project's progress. It was midmorning when he returned to the small trailer that served as his on-site office. He tossed his hard hat on a dented file cabinet and massaged his aching head. The doctor had told him to stay flat for a few days, but then the doctor didn't face construction deadlines and a contract penalty clause rich enough to retire the national debt.

Besides, Steven had toughed out worse injuries. After a skiing mishap, he'd hobbled around the job site in an ankle-to-thigh cast that had amused his unsympathetic crew immensely. Steven had taken the good-natured ribbing in stride, particularly since the damage had occurred during one of his rare forays into the social scene.

Sliding over an icy mountain hadn't really been Steven's idea of a swell time to begin with, but a friend had introduced him to an attractive redheaded ski bunny and for a few disastrous days, Steven had suppressed his uncle's warnings and his own hard-earned lessons on romantic pitfalls.

Those lessons had been quickly reinforced. The young lady in question had murmured empathetically, drawn garish pink hearts on his cast, then headed up the slopes with a healthier specimen of virile manhood. Steven had moped by the lodge fireplace licking his wounds and recalling an even more painful feminine betrayal.

Now Steven shook off the unpleasant memories and stared glumly at the small cylinder of pain medication. The construction site was dangerous enough without numbing one's senses, so he reluctantly settled on an aspirin then picked up the telephone and dialed his uncle's number.

After several rings, Steven was relieved to hear Edison's voice. They chatted for a few moments, nonchalant banter about the weather and such. Then Steven approached the subject of his call with what he hoped was convincing casualness. "By the way, do you remember that lovely hillside home you were interested in a few months ago?"

There was a slight pause before Edison responded. "No, can't say that I do. But then, we must have seen a hundred pieces of property before I finally moved into my apartment."

Steven grimaced, unable to understand why Edison had decided on such a noisy, crowded apartment complex in the first place. His uncle could afford so much better. Steven had seen to that.

Now Steven hoped that with a few well-placed reminders, Edison would realize that the good life was still available. "This particular home was a brick-and-stucco one-story at the end of a quiet cul-de-sac. Do you remember? There was a pool with matching jacuzzi, a shaded deck and huge garden area. You said it suited you because the kitchen was small and the bedroom had a huge corner fireplace."

Edison chuckled. "Well, I can't cook and I figured that since these weary bones are too old to work, they might as well be warm and rested."

"So you remember the place?"

"Umm. I sure as hell remember the price."

"The market has changed. In fact, I just spoke to the realtor this morning and not only is that property still available, the price has dropped nearly twenty percent."

After a long moment of silence, Edison spoke again. "I'm quite happy where I am, son."

"But a place of your own would give you privacy—"

"If I want privacy, I can lock my door."

Frustrated, Steven drummed on his desk. The debate wasn't going well so he decided to pull out all the stops and shamelessly exploit one of his uncle's passions. "Wouldn't you love to have a huge garden instead of one potted tomato on a six-foot patio?"

Edison chuckled. "I've already got my garden, almost an acre planted and another one ready to cultivate."

"What?" The news deflated Steven completely. "Where?"

Edison's voice fairly shook with enthusiasm. "Hettie talked the complex owners into letting us work the weed bank behind the main building. The lettuce is nearly picking size and we've got cabbage, peas and cauliflower coming up, too. The broccoli doesn't look too good, though. Bugs. Hettie says they're cabbage maggots."

Hettie says.

Steven swallowed a sharp retort. "Ah, isn't two acres a bit much for two people?"

"Oh, there's about twenty of us working it. We're going to distribute the harvest to the poor old folks who can't afford fresh vegetables."

"How commendable." Steven massaged his throbbing head. This wasn't going well at all.

Dismissing Steven's dry retort, Edison spoke with obvious pride. "It's our duty to help people who are down on their luck. Hettie says..."

With a disgusted snort, Steven tuned out the Gospel According to Hettie, swiveled his chair around and stared glassy-eyed out the window. There was no doubt in his mind that Edison was totally smitten. How could this have happened? Emotional entanglements inevitably led to disaster, a fact Edison had repeatedly drummed into Steven over the years.

And through his own parents' tumultuous marriage, Steven had seen the truth in Edison's philosophy. When the screaming fights had become unbearable, young Stevie had turned to Edison for comfort.

"It's not your daddy's fault," Edison had told him. "Nor your momma's, either. Marriage just seems to make people crazy. You can't blame them."

But Stevie had blamed them. He'd blamed his father for drinking away the rent money. He'd blamed his mother for her envy and desire for material wealth. He'd blamed himself for not being a good enough child to make either of them happy.

And when they'd died in the flaming wreckage of their battered old car, Stevie had blamed himself for that, too.

At eight, Stevie had suddenly been an orphan, having lost everyone he'd ever cared about, except one—his bachelor uncle. Edison alone had taken in the despondent child, nurtured him, loved him and turned him into a strong, capable man. Edison's strength and devotion had saved Steven's sanity. Through the years, they had developed a deep and loving bond, a commitment that never wavered. Edison had been the only person on earth that Stevie could trust.

That hadn't changed. But now it was Edison who needed protection.

As Steven's mind returned to the present, he waited for a pause in Edison's exuberant monologue and quickly changed the subject. "How about dinner tonight? My treat."

"I can't," Edison said cheerfully. "Hettie and I are going to catch a bite before choir practice."

"Choir practice?" That was a new wrinkle.

"Yep. I can't carry a tune in a bucket but Hettie says I'm loud enough to make up for that."

Steven cleared his throat. "You seem to be spending quite a bit of time with Mrs. Gregory."

"Finest woman I've ever met," Edison replied reverently.

"I'm sure she's very nice." Steven wasn't sure at all but something in his uncle's rapturous tone warned that criticizing Hettie would not be prudent. "Of course, you haven't known her very long," Steven added cautiously.

"Long enough." A contented sigh filtered over the line. "Women like that make a man start to wonder..." Edison's voice trailed away.

Steven was instantly alert. "Wonder about what?"

"Oh, just about my life and how things might have been different. I've been a pretty selfish guy, you know."

Steven found that statement ridiculous and said so. "A selfish man doesn't raise his brother's son without expecting so much as a thank you."

"You don't understand. I've always judged myself on monetary values and I never minded looking down on people who didn't meet my standards. Now I've finally realized that money just isn't that important."

Steven felt a chill run down his spine. "Money is damned important, particularly if you don't have any."

"That's the point, son. There's so many people who have nothing and I have so much more than I need."

"Is that what Hettie says?" Steven asked coldly. The direction of the conversation seemed a sick confirmation of his deepest suspicions. Steven thought of the apple-cheeked con artist defrauding gullible old men out of their life's savings. "And does Hettie have any ideas on how you can relieve yourself of this excess wealth?"

A strained silence fell over the line, then Edison deftly changed the subject. "Say, how was the ball game?"

Steven considered pressing the subject of Hettie's monetary philosophy, then decided that he'd get better information from a less biased source. He sighed. "Let's just say that the game was enlightening."

"Who won?"

"I haven't a clue. We left early."

That information seemed to tickle Edison. Steven suspected his uncle had totally misinterpreted the reason for their early departure. Edison's next comment confirmed that. "Lenore's a lovely girl, don't you think?"

"What I think is that someone should warn the pentagon. The woman has more destructive power than a nuclear warhead."

Edison chuckled. "She's just like her grandma."

That was a frightening thought.

"It's nice that you showed her a good time," Edison told him. "Hettie says Lenore works too hard and worries too much. The poor girl has had it kind of rough since her husband died."

"Died?" Steven's fingers tightened on the receiver. Although Edison had initially mentioned that Lenore had been married, Steven had assumed that the relationship had ended naturally—through divorce. He frowned. Death was quite another matter and he felt a surge of sympathy, remembering how quiet she'd become when they'd left the clinic.

Still he couldn't afford to become all mushy about this. People died. It was sad, but that was simply the way of things. Edison was Steven's primary concern now and his only interest in Lenore was to discover what, if anything, she had to do with Hester Gregory's suspicious interest in his uncle.

And by God, Steven was going to do just that.

Lenore's Happy Lamb Preschool was located in a refurbished Victorian bordering the city's tough south side. Fiber board cutouts of too-cute animals decorated the front of the two-story building and peering beyond the pastel clapboards, Steven saw the roomy rear yard was a tangle of freshly painted swing sets and jungle gyms.

Tucked between graffiti-marred fences and unkempt houses, the tidy establishment seemed out of place. Steven stepped from his car, glanced down the weed-choked block, and wondered if his tires would be gone when he returned. Hell of a neighborhood for a day-care center, he decided and wondered what kind of parents would leave their children in such an unsavory environment.

Judging by the noise emanating from the place, there were apparently quite a few such parents. Childish squeals greeted Steven before he'd even reached the front door of Lenore's day-care center. He paused, empty thermos in hand, and tried to gather his thoughts. The direct approach wouldn't work. Few people would take kindly to a demand for audited financials and personal references. Besides, someone involved in a fraudulent scam wouldn't think twice about forging such documents.

Not that Steven honestly believed Hettie or Lenore were actually a pair of seasoned con artists, but where his uncle was concerned there was simply no such thing as too much caution. And Steven was well aware that a lack of illegal activities didn't preclude other ulterior and detrimental motives. Edison, like Old Crazy Sam, was simply too trusting, too blinded by dreams.

Resolutely mounting the steps, Steven knocked and heard bedlam behind the pink enamel doors. He started to knock again, then noticed a sign that read, Please Come In.

Great. The foolish woman even left the door unlocked so any mugger could stroll inside. Muttering to himself, Steven twisted the knob and stepped into absolute chaos.

"Eeeek! Watch out, mister! You're gonna squish him."

Steven froze as a mop-headed youngster dived in front of his feet, fat little arms outstretched and fingers grasping at some invisible prey. The child slid into a closed door at the end of the foyer and was instantly surrounded by a gaggle of his little peers.

"Is he in the closet?" asked one breathless youngster.

A freckle-faced boy stood by holding a large coffee can. "Open the door! When he runs out, I'll trap him."

"No, silly. You'll scare him."

From another room came a burst of squeals and the sound of scampering feet. "I got one! I got one!"

"Wonderful, Luther. Now put him back into the cage."

Was that Lenore's voice?

Before Steven could turn toward the familiar sound, one of the children opened the closet door and a tiny ball of fur shot out of the darkness and scampered across Steven's shoe. With a simultaneous scream of delight, the entire group of youngsters dashed after the creature.

After his heart returned to normal, Steven followed. The sight that greeted him should have been shocking but this was, after all, Lenore's class. Steven had been prepared for anything, even the sight of two dozen children screaming wildly and diving under colorful plastic furniture.

Something fuzzy dashed across the shiny checkerboard floor and was chased by two giggling little girls. He saw two teenage girls coordinating the mayhem along with a middle-aged blond woman, who was clutching a toddler under one arm as she scanned the floor with obvious apprehension.

Then in the midst of this pandemonium, Steven finally spotted Lenore, skirt climbing her shapely legs as she bent awkwardly, struggling to retrieve something from behind a pink-and-purple bookcase.

"Gotcha!" she mumbled. When she straightened, Steven saw a furry ball cupped in her palms. She walked briskly across the room and carefully deposited her catch in a large glass terrarium filled with other wiggling creatures. Lenore then glanced around and called out to no one in particular, "There are still two missing, kids. Joey, Heather...will you please check the kitchen? But for heaven sake don't tell the cook what you're looking for—Steven!"

The light in her eyes when she saw him did peculiar things to his stomach and he found himself hoping that she'd smile so he could see that ridiculous dimple again.

She did. "This is an unexpected surprise."

"For me, too," Steven responded, watching the screaming mass of children.

"It's the gerbils," Lenore explained. "Danny left the cage open again and—" Suddenly she dashed over to a diapered toddler. "No-no, dear. Gerbils don't taste good. Here, let's put him away, all right?"

When the crisis had been resolved, Lenore returned, cheeks flushed and hair mussed, as though she'd just tumbled out of bed. At that moment, she seemed the most desirable woman Steven had ever seen. He was mesmerized, staring at her moving lips for several seconds before he realized that she'd been speaking to him.

He cleared his throat. "Excuse me?"

"I asked what you were doing here."

"I, ah, wanted to return this." He stiffly held out the thermos.

She accepted it and scrutinized his jaw. "The swelling seems to have gone down considerably. You kept using the ice packs, didn't you? That's probably what did the trick. How was the soup?"

Steven's head was spinning. "Fine. I mean, very fine...er, very good. Thank you."

"You're welcome."

During the awkward pause that followed, Steven tugged at his collar and Lenore stared at her shoes. Finally Steven took a deep breath. "Since I owe you lunch, I'd hoped that you—"

A tubby child of about four suddenly appeared at Lenore's side. "Mrs. Lange wants to see you."

"Good grief! Did one of the gerbils find its way into the bookkeeper's office?"

The boy shrugged. "She jus' said I should tell you to come."

Lenore smoothed the child's blond hair. "Thank you for the message, Justin. I'll go see her right away." Satisfied, the child tottled off and Lenore returned her attention to Steven. "Sorry for the interruption. Now, what were you saying?"

From the corner of his eye, Steven saw two more children heading their way and was determined to complete his mission before the next wave of intruders. "I'd like to take you to lunch," he blurted quickly and none too soon, as the final words were nearly drowned out as the chattering horde swooped into the room imprisoning the adults in a circle of squirming, squealing excitement.

To Steven's surprise, Lenore simply put one finger to her lips and the children instantly fell silent. Then she looked at Steven as though his skull were glass and she could read every thought. He shifted uncomfortably awaiting her answer.

She pursed her lips as though considering the implication of his invitation and Steven was certain that she was psychically attuned to his subversive intent. Finally she spoke. "Can you wait about fifteen minutes?"

He managed a stiff smile. "Sure."

After another penetrating look, Lenore glanced over her shoulder and spoke to the harried blonde. "Maggie, I'm going to see Mrs. Lange for a few moments and then I'll be going out for a while. Can you handle the kids' lunch?"

Maggie looked as though she'd prefer to be staked out on an ant hill but simply mumbled, "Certainly," then dashed toward a little boy who had decided to finger-paint his own shirt.

Bending slightly, Lenore spoke to the cluster of youngsters gathered around her. "All right now, children. I want all of you to form your wash-up line and get ready for lunch, okay?"

A simultaneous chorus rose. "Okay!" Then the giggling youngsters scurried down the hallway. Lenore straightened and smoothed her crisp peach linen skirt. "Can I get you something while you're waiting... coffee, iced tea?"

"No, I'm fine, thanks."

"I shouldn't be long."

"Take your time," Steven said magnanimously. "Business comes first."

She regarded him pensively, then nodded and walked quickly across the foyer. Steven watched as she went down the hall and turned into the first open doorway. He heard a woman's voice, not Lenore's, and noted that the hushed conversation seemed strained and somewhat tense. Edging casually toward the hallway, he situated himself at the furthest corner of the foyer and listened intently. The voices were too muffled to identify any specific topic of discussion. After a moment, he was shocked to realize that his ear was nearly pressed against the wall as he strained to interpret each muted word.

Instantly he straightened, disgusted by the blatant invasion of her privacy. Steven was far from a saint. In fact, on more than one occasion he'd stretched the realm of social—and perhaps even legal—acceptability in the blind pursuit of a righteous cause.

Still, skulking around and eavesdropping on private conversations was just too distasteful. First he'd try to get what he needed directly, from Lenore herself. If that failed, well, he'd do whatever was necessary, distasteful or not.

He hoped it wouldn't come to that.

Inside the pleasant café, Lenore stared at the menu as though she was really interested in lunch. Actually, she wasn't the least bit hungry and couldn't quite understand why she'd accepted Steven's invitation. Curiosity, probably, and an abhorrence of being rude. Still, she shouldn't have left poor Maggie alone.

Steven's voice startled her. "Have you decided yet?"

Lenore blinked, wondering how he could have known she was trying to figure out what she was doing here. Then she noticed the waitress with pencil poised. "Oh. Yes, well, I'll have whatever you're having."

He eyed her for a moment, then dictated their orders. The waitress left and Steven continued to watch Lenore. For some reason, the intense scrutiny made her nervous. She absently fiddled with a fork, wondering why she couldn't think of anything to say. Being struck speechless was a rare and uncomfortable occurrence for Lenore, but here she was, squirming like a toddler in church.

Finally Steven broke the tense silence. "Are you feeling better?"

The question surprised her. "I'm fine. Why do you ask?"

He shrugged nonchalantly. "You seemed upset after your meeting with the bookkeeper, that's all."

Lenore was surprised at the astute observation and annoyed that her concern had been so obvious. Now she managed a too-bright smile. "All those silly debits and credits just confuse the devil out of me," she lied. "Poor Mrs. Lange does her best to enlighten me but one look at all those numbered columns and my brain starts to spin."

Steven hiked a brow but didn't press the subject. Instead, he asked, "What made you decide to open a day-care center?"

"Actually the entire thing was my grandmother's idea."

That seemed of particular interest to Steven. He leaned forward, encouraging her with a murmured, "Really?"

"Yes. When Grandma was a volunteer at the local welfare office, she realized that most of the women were struggling single mothers in a catch-twenty-two situation. They couldn't afford child care, so they couldn't work. If they couldn't work, they couldn't afford child care."

"So you decided to take care of other people's children, just like that?" He snapped his fingers for emphasis and Lenore was amused by his obvious skepticism.

"It wasn't quite that impulsive," she assured him. "I had always wanted to work with children. Initially I wanted to be a teacher and had nearly completed my master's degree in education."

"Teaching is a noble profession. What changed your mind?"

Lenore's smile faded and she glanced out the sunny window. Grief had changed her mind. For months after Michael's death, Lenore had existed in a surrealistic haze, unable to eat or to sleep or to concentrate on anything except her own primal pain and the sickness in her soul. The career she'd prepared for no longer mattered. Nothing had mattered. Lenore had dropped out of life.

But she didn't tell Steven any of this. Instead of answering his question directly, she opted for a more circuitous route. "Grandma introduced me to one particular woman who had just survived an abusive relationship and a shattering divorce," Lenore said quietly. "The poor lady was desperately trying to put her life back together and I agreed to care for her two children. A few weeks later, Grandma introduced me to another woman in a similar situation and the rest, as they say..." Lenore smiled and spread her hands dramatically.

As he considered this information, Steven made a production of arranging the napkin in his lap. "I thought you said that these women couldn't afford child care."

"When they were out of work, I didn't charge them. They paid what they could."

"That doesn't sound like very good business."

"Probably not but at the time, I was motivated more by the children than building a cushy bank account." The waitress appeared with their salads and Lenore leaned back to allow the woman access to the table.

Impatiently drumming his fingers on the table, Steven could hardly contain himself until the waitress had completed her appointed task and left their table. Lenore had barely picked up her fork when Steven asked, "So money wasn't an issue?"

Although he made a valiant attempt to sound casual, Lenore suspected the question had a deeper motivation, although she was puzzled as to what that might be. She tasted a bland bite of lettuce and regarded him quietly. He was as tense as an overwound spring and she wondered why. Finally she answered simply. "Money is always an issue."

That didn't appear to be the answer he wanted. Steven's dark brows furrowed and his mouth thinned into a hard line. For several moments, he poked listlessly at his meal. "Tell me about your grandmother," he said suddenly.

Lenore's fork froze in midair. "Why?"

"She's a very interesting woman and my uncle is . . . fond of her."

Relaxing, Lenore laughed. "Everyone is fond of Grandma. She's one of a kind. What do you want to know?"

"Does she still work for the welfare office?"

"She never actually worked for them. She was an unpaid volunteer and yes, they still call her occasionally to counsel some of their clients, but Grandma's got so many irons in the fire now that it's difficult for her to find enough time."

"What kinds of 'irons'?"

"Well, let's see now." Lenore laid down her fork and began to count on her fingers. "There's the Meals-on-Wheels program—that's one of her favorites because she has a chance to chat with folks who are closed in all day—and she's active in the local senior citizen center...umm, oh, there's also her church choir practice and she's executive director of A.S.F.P.R."

Steven blinked. "A.S.F.P.R.?"

"Active Seniors For Political Reform," Lenore said innocently, biting back a smile. "You might be familiar with some of their lobbying efforts."

Steven straightened in his seat and his eyes narrowed. "The jail-house rabble-rousers."

"Grandma prefers to consider the organization a watchdog for citizen's rights, but I suppose that's a picky point," Lenore replied lightly, both confused and amused by Steven's seriousness. You'd think by his dark scowl that they were discussing the advent of war rather than the harmless activities of a gray-haired old lady.

Then Steven leaned back, arms folded and expression grim. "So with all this leisure time available, your grandmother must be financially secure."

"I beg your pardon?"

Steven squirmed under her incredulous stare. "That sounded rather rude. What I meant is simply that since Hettie has so much time available for volunteer activities, her husband must have left her rather well-off..." His voice trailed away and he had the grace to look embarrassed.

Although Lenore wasn't angered by the personal nature of his assumptions, she was no longer amused. Pushing her plate away, she propped her forearms on the table and met Steven's sheepish glance. "My grandmother is far from rich," she replied coolly. "She lives on social security and a small pension inherited from my grandfather. Now I'd like to know exactly what business my family's financial affairs are to you."

Steven pursed his lips thoughtfully. "I'm sorry if I've offended you."

"You haven't offended me. You've annoyed me."

He shrugged. "That wasn't my intent. Sometimes I tend to be a bit blunt."

Somewhat mollified, Lenore still wasn't satisfied. "So why the third degree? Is your uncle in the market for a rich widow?" Lenore had been joking, of course, but Steven's head snapped up and she instantly realized that she'd inadvertently touched a nerve. She was stunned. "That's it, isn't it? You're trying to set Edison up with my grandmother?"

"Good Lord, no!" Steven was obviously horrified by the thought.

"Then what on earth is this all about?"

Steven sighed. "Surely you must realize that Edison and Hettie have been spending a great deal of time together."

"They're friends. So what?"

"I think more than friendship is involved." He raked his hair in frustration, then absently scratched at the tablecloth and avoided Lenore's eyes. "I believe that this... friendship is emerging into something more, well, intimate."

Lenore sat ramrod stiff, gaping like a grounded fish. Finally she managed to sputter, "You're out of your mind. I don't know whether to laugh in your face or pour ice water in your lap. How dare you imply that two sweet old people could behave in such a sordid manner?"

"I'm not insinuating that a sexual relationship is sordid. They are adults, after all."

Sexual relationship!

The concept absolutely blew Lenore's mind.

Suppressing a disquieting recollection of how Hettie had watched Edison with glowing eyes, Lenore waved away Steven's concerns as one might swat at a pesky fly. "My grandparents were married for almost fifty years. They adored each other. Why, Grandma would no more look at another man... that way... than jump off the moon. The entire notion is positively absurd."

Slowly Steven shook his head. "You can't be that naive."

"I'm not naive. I'm realistic." Lenore bristled at the pity in his eyes. "Grandma loved my grandfather. She'd never betray him. But if you're so darned worried about it, why in the devil don't you just talk to your uncle?"

"I've tried," Steven said miserably. "But Edison's completely inexperienced in . . . these matters."

"Inexperienced? Excuse me, but the man is almost eighty years old."

"True, but he's been a bachelor all his life."

"Surely he's had relationships."

"He never had a dearth of feminine companionship, if that's what you mean. But to my uncle, business always came first and as far as I know, he was never seriously involved with anyone."

"Then what's the big deal, here? If he's managed to survive this long without being hooked, he's obviously developed some immunity. I honestly don't understand your concern."

Steven considered her comment thoughtfully. Finally he sighed. "I don't understand, either. I just know that something is going on between my uncle and your grandmother and I don't like it one damned bit."

Lenore folded her arms tightly. Actually Edison was rather handsome and dashing, with the vigor of a man half his age. She silently admitted that the seniors *had* been spending a lot of time together and she even recalled seeing a bouquet of roses in her grandmother's room.

But none of that meant anything.

Lenore dabbed her face with the cool linen napkin and convinced herself that Steven's bizarre speculation was absolutely ridiculous. She wanted to laugh in his face but couldn't make a sound. Secret doubt clogged her throat and cold fear squeezed her heart. Steven had to be wrong.

But what if he wasn't?

Chapter Four

"Mrs. Blaine, you simply can't allow this to continue."
The bookkeeper's squinty half glasses fell from her nose and
dangled by a jeweled cord. "As things stand now you'll
barely make this week's payroll and last month's rent is now
two weeks overdue. You simply must cut back on the *pro-bono* enrollment."

Lenore nodded respectfully. "I understand your concern, Mrs. Lange, but I can't simply toss these children out
because their parents are temporarily unable to pay our
standard fees."

"Unemployed parents do not require child care."

"Well, they certainly can't search for a job carrying their
kids in a backpack." Lenore stood quickly and laid a warm
hand on the woman's rigid shoulder. "Everything will work
out. It always does."

Mrs. Lange was unconvinced. "I realize how deeply you
care for these children . . . really I do. But I would be dere-
lict in my responsibilities if I didn't inform you that the
center is nearly insolvent. If you don't get that bank loan, I
doubt you'll be able to keep the doors open for more than a
month."

Somehow Lenore managed to maintain a calm expression and didn't mention that the loan in question had already been denied. There was no sense worrying the poor woman. Besides, there were other banks.

As Mrs. Lange continued her depressing diatribe, Lenore pretended to listen politely but her mind wandered. She wished Michael was here. He'd know what to do. First he'd scowl, considering all the feasible options and eventually, he'd come up with a foolproof plan. She could almost picture him standing beside her, dark hair mussed by the constant plowing by impatient fingers, his green eyes narrowed in concentration...

Wait a minute. Lenore blinked at the mental image. Michael had blond hair. Shocked, Lenore suddenly realized that she'd been thinking not of Michael, but of Steven Collier. Had she gone mad?

Standing quickly, Lenore ignored the bookkeeper's startled gasp. "Thank you so much for your help," she told the stunned woman. "I'll take your suggestions under consideration and we'll discuss them in detail next week."

Using the desk as a prop, Mrs. Lange pushed herself into a standing position. "Uh, well, I'll be here on Wednesday as usual. Perhaps—"

"Absolutely," Lenore interrupted smoothly. "We'll talk then."

In less than two minutes, Lenore was alone in the deserted center. She turned off the lights and, purse in hand, stood quietly in the darkness. Why had she imagined Steven Collier's face when she'd been thinking about her husband? Absently touching her barren ring finger, Lenore focused on the obscure part of her past and was frustrated. The memories should be so clear but like her beautiful wedding ring, they had disappeared without her permission, another unwilling betrayal of the man she had once loved.

Again she squeezed her eyes closed, trying to picture his face. The only image she could conjure was from the photograph on her living room table. She couldn't remember how he laughed. She couldn't remember the feel of his skin beneath her fingers and she couldn't remember if her own heart had leaped at his touch.

Of course it had. She *had* loved Michael. She still did. And Lenore was just as certain that Hettie still loved Grandpa. Death couldn't erase love, and time couldn't ease the terrible grief of having lost that love. Even if her grandmother had feelings for Edison—and Lenore wasn't willing to concede that possibility—Hettie had suffered too much grief, too dear a loss. To become emotionally involved would be to risk having her heart ripped out again. Hester Gregory would never put herself in such jeopardy again. No sane person would.

So Steven Collier's tawdry speculations had to be the delusions of an overzealous mind.

By the time Lenore had walked to her car, she had convinced herself that Steven's theory was more entertaining than insulting. Certainly Grandma would get a giggle out of being considered a femme fatale. Lenore smiled, imagining how Hettie would probably hoot gleefully at the asinine notion, then perform a hilarious imitation of a sultry fan dancer.

Hettie was such a kick.

As Lenore drove onto the freeway, she decided to stop by her grandmother's apartment and relay the day's events. After all, Hettie was always in the mood for a funny story.

In less than ten minutes she was in the carpeted corridor outside the door of her grandmother's apartment. She simultaneously knocked and glanced at her watch, satisfied that nine o'clock was late enough for Hettie to be back from her various activities yet too early for her grandmother to have retired for the night. After a moment, Lenore knocked again and called softly. "Grandma? Are you still awake?"

The muffled scurry of rushing feet emanated from behind the closed door. Lenore frowned, listening. She heard whispered voices and thought that rather strange. Perhaps Hettie was holding some kind of meeting, although it was a bit late for that.

Suddenly the door opened slightly and Hettie peered out. "Lenore, dear. I...wasn't expecting you." The older woman's cheeks were flushed and her eyes were even brighter than usual. Hettie spoke with a breathless quality that was uncharacteristic and quite peculiar.

Lenore regarded her grandmother for a moment. "I just dropped by for a couple of minutes. I didn't think you'd be going to bed so early."

"Bed? Oh, heavens no, child." Hettie's laugh was oddly strained. Releasing the doorknob, she tugged at the nape of her fuzzy bathrobe with one hand and patted her red face with the other. Lenore noticed that her grandmother's hair was damp, as though she'd just showered. Then the door yawned open and Lenore glimpsed a movement inside the apartment and assumed it to be Buster, Hettie's cranky tomcat. Lenore peered around her agitated grandmother for a better look and nearly fainted.

There was Edison Collier, sitting on her grandmother's sofa, wearing a bathrobe and a sheepish grin.

The old man cleared his throat, tugged at his earlobe and tried vainly to cover the bony knees exposed by his short terry-cloth robe. Finally he managed a thin greeting. "Good evening, Lenore. It's, ah, nice to see you again."

All Lenore could do was nod stupidly. She clutched her purse so tightly that her fingers ached and she sagged against the door frame, her head spinning. "I didn't mean to intrude," she mumbled lamely.

"Intrude?" Hettie's high-pitched laugh was a bit too bright. "Nonsense, child. It's always a delight to see you. Come in."

Stepping back, Hettie opened the door and took hold of Lenore's stiff arm, coaxing her inside. Lenore licked her dry lips and glanced quickly around the neat living room. Soft music floated from the compact stereo and on the coffee table was a bottle of chilled champagne along with two crystal goblets.

It was a scene right out of *The Seduction* and for a moment Lenore wanted nothing more than to crawl up Edison's scrawny chest and pluck out his mustache one whisker at a time. How dare he try to take advantage of her grandmother?

"Try" was the operative word here because in spite of evidence to the contrary, Lenore was certain that this sordid scenario had been entirely Edison's idea. After all, poor Hettie had spent a lifetime with only one man and was painfully naive about romantic liaisons.

Lenore fixed Edison with a furious stare. He cringed visibly and Hettie hastened to his defense. "I know this looks a bit awkward, dear." She tittered nervously and blushed to the roots of her damp gray hair. "It's just that we haven't had a chance to dry off yet."

Lenore nearly went into shock. *We?* They had both been wet? At the same time? "I...beg your pardon?"

Wringing her plump hands, Hettie launched into an overly zealous explanation. "Sonny took me to this lovely restaurant up in Malibu...oh my, you should try this place. There's a marvelous balcony overlooking the ocean and when the waves break on the rocks, you can actually feel the spray. When you go, you simply must try the *mahi-mahi* and...what did you have, Sonny?" The old man opened his mouth but before he could respond Hettie snapped her fingers. "Scampi in garlic sauce, right dear?" Edison didn't even bother to nod because Hettie was off and running again. "No matter. Anyway, it was so lovely that after our meal, Sonny and I took a walk on the beach. Well, I simply wasn't watching where I was going—you know how distracted I get—and this huge wave came out of nowhere and just about knocked me out of my shoes." Hettie punctuated this news flash with a melodramatic sigh.

Lenore was instantly concerned. "Were you hurt?"

"Sonny rescued me, didn't you, dear?" Hettie gazed warmly at Edison, who simply bobbed his head and grinned foolishly. "He was really quite gallant."

Folding her arms, Lenore frowned. "Chivalry seems to run in the family."

Hettie ignored Lenore's wry comment and continued her story. "After Sonny pulled me out, we were both soaked to the skin and cold. Oh, my dear, you can't imagine how chilled we were. Why, Sonny's nose turned absolutely blue and I was shivering so hard, I nearly shook my girdle off."

As Hettie chuckled in delight, Lenore was still suspicious. Her grandmother had not yet explained why Edison couldn't dry off in his own apartment.

In less than a minute, Hettie answered the unspoken question. "Well, Sonny and I decided we might as well be wet and warm as wet and cold, so we changed into our swimsuits and took a nice, hot soak in the complex jacuzzi."

"Swimsuits?" Relief flooded every pore of Lenore's body as she noticed the familiar flowered bodice peeking from beneath her grandmother's robe. Suddenly Lenore was flustered and embarrassed that she'd suffered even a moment's doubt.

But Lenore wasn't the only flustered person here. Her grandmother was still talking much too fast and Lenore noticed a rosy flush staining Hettie's round cheeks. "Sonny and I were just having a taste of champagne…warms up the inside, you know…would you care to join us?"

Lenore tried to smile but her lips stuck to her teeth. "No, thank you. I should be going."

"Nonsense. You've just arrived."

"No, really. It's late. I'll call you tomorrow."

Giving Hettie a quick hug, Lenore kissed her grandmother's cheek, mumbled a polite farewell to Edison and managed to edge out the door. By the time Lenore returned to the parking lot and slid into her car, she was totally befuddled by the apparent contradictions. Since Hettie didn't have a dishonest bone in her round, little body, Lenore was certain that her grandmother's explanation—as far as it went—had been truthful.

Still, something seemed amiss and Lenore was deeply concerned. In spite of Hettie's political savvy, the older woman didn't know squat about men and why should she? Hettie had been a teenager when she'd married Grandpa, and Lenore knew that since that day, there had never been another man in her grandmother's life. Nor would there be. Lenore was certain of that, too, because she and Hettie shared something that went beyond the kinship of blood.

They shared the same agonizing loss.

Lenore could remember every detail of that day six years ago. It was strange to recall something so tragic with such clarity when all that came before was vague and unfocused. Even now she could still smell the sickening floral fragrance as Michael's casket had been lowered into the damp earth.

Through that traumatic event, Hettie had been the tower of strength. Lenore remembered that after the mourners departed, her grandmother had stayed on to prepare the magic elixer on which the older woman had relied for decades—a steaming pot of herb tea.

Lenore had listlessly refused the offering. "I don't want anything."

"It will make you feel better, child."

Closing her eyes, Lenore simply shook her head. Nothing could make her feel better. Nothing could make her feel anything, ever again. She was hollow. An integral part of her soul had been buried with her husband and life was over. The fact that Lenore was still breathing and that her heart continued to beat was simply a biological accident. Michael was gone. There was nothing left.

Hettie understood. "The pain will ease, dear. It will take time but eventually, you'll watch the sunrise and feel joy at its beauty."

"It hurts so much," Lenore whispered.

"I know, child. I know." Hettie gathered Lenore in her plump arms, comforting her. "You don't have to be brave now. It's all right to cry."

"I can't. I . . . don't have any tears."

Holding Lenore's head against her breast, Hettie kissed her granddaughter's head and rocked her as though she were a child. Lenore closed her eyes and allowed herself to feel safe, if only for that moment. Her grandmother's words were distant, unintelligible, but Lenore was comforted by the familiar soothing sound. Finally Lenore spoke. "Grandma?"

"Yes, dear?"

"When Grandpa died, did you feel . . . empty inside?"

After a moment, Hettie answered in a tight whisper. "Yes."

Reluctantly Lenore left the warmth of her grandmother's arms and sat up. "How did you live with it?"

Hettie touched Lenore's cheek and managed a loving smile. "I loved your grandfather very, very much. When I lost him, I felt as though my entire world had been shattered. He was everything to me and without him, I didn't feel as though I could go on."

"But you *did* go on. You survived."

Brushing a strand of hair from Lenore's face, Hettie nodded somberly. "Losing someone you love is the worst pain in the world. At first, I felt like you do now...as though I'd lost my capacity to ever love again. Then I realized that how ever much I had lost, I still had so much left. I had my children and I had you. And as time went on, I learned that the love I felt for others was still inside me, it had just been buried for a little while. The wounds are deep and take time to heal."

"Did you heal, Grandma?" Lenore asked softly.

Hettie looked away and Lenore recognized her torment. Although her grandmother never replied, Lenore already knew the answer. No one could ever be completely healed from such agonizing loss.

The message had been clear. Love equaled vulnerability, the risk of emotional devastation and hideous pain. That had been one lesson that Lenore had never forgotten.

Now, she sat alone in the darkness and prayed that her grandmother hadn't forgotten, either.

"Thanks, Jerry. I owe you one." Steven cradled the receiver and glanced out the window at the bustling construction site. Over the past week, he'd pulled every string possible in a covert quest for information on Hettie and Lenore. Although he hadn't unearthed anything particularly sinister, some of the facts he'd discovered were a bit disquieting.

His conversation with Jerry Liman had been the most enlightening—and the most disturbing.

Steven had met Jerry at Chamber of Commerce meetings and over the years, they'd become routine business associates. Jerry's bank had financed many of Collier Development's most successful projects, including the professional office complex now under construction.

Jerry was a consummate banking professional who would never breach client confidentiality or divulge privileged financial information. Still Steven hadn't gotten to the top of a cut-throat, competitive business without learning how to straddle a fine ethical line. By vaguely implying interest in a potential development deal at The Happy Lamb site, Steven discovered that Hester Gregory co-owned Lenore's day-care center. That had been an interesting revelation but Jerry's next tidbit of info turned out to be the bombshell.

To say the center was financially troubled was an understatement. From what Steven could gather from Liman's bleak assessment, The Happy Lamb was heavily mortgaged and Lenore's request for refinancing had just been denied because of decreased revenue projections. In fact, Steven had gotten the distinct impression that without an immediate source of capital, the center would be teetering on the brink of bankruptcy.

Frowning, Steven tapped a pencil on his desk and glumly realized that his uncle's nest egg could present one hell of a temptation to anyone in such dire financial straits.

Money talked. No, money shouted and turned otherwise sane, God-fearing people into devious monsters, willing to sell their souls for a taste of the good life. Steven had seen firsthand how the lack and desire for material wealth had destroyed his parents' bitter marriage and caused the disintegration of so many other relationships.

Only Edison had miraculously avoided the inevitable disillusionment of wedded bliss, having accurately pegged that staid institution for what it truly was—people using each other to further their own social and economical goals.

At first Steven had balked at the cynical assessment but had listened politely out of respect. Then he'd met Lucinda Marks and all of Edison's dire warnings had been swept away in a wave of passion. Steven had loved that woman desperately. Blinded by desire, he'd conjured foolish images of a white picket fence, a gaggle of giggling kids...the whole nine yards. The day Lucinda agreed to marry him had been the happiest day of his life.

When Steven had discovered his beautiful fiancée entertaining her wealthy new lover, he'd been devastated.

Lucinda had been sorry, of course. She hadn't wanted to hurt him but had blandly explained that a woman like her needed certain advantages in life. Since Steven continued to pour his assets back into his business, she just didn't believe he could afford her.

Thanks to Lucinda, Edison's warnings had finally struck home. Relationships, Steven learned, were like the stock market—volatile, unpredictable and economically driven.

Now, Steven feared his uncle's emotional resolve, unshakable for nearly eight decades, was weakening and he was worried sick. Edison was too old, too emotionally fragile to survive a similar betrayal.

Although the evidence continued to mount, there was no specific proof of Hester Gregory's deceitful intent. Still, the information Steven had gleaned so far definitely gave credence to his suspicions. Worse, he'd learned that Lenore and Hettie's professional and personal life were intertwined tighter than braided hemp. If Hettie was pulling some kind of scam, Lenore was involved up to her svelte little derriere and that thought literally made Steven ill. He remembered her delightful, unaffected laugh and the way that silly dimple lit up her entire face. There was an intrinsic reality to the woman, an aura of purity that could almost make a believer out of him. Almost.

Trust was a fool's weakness and Steven was no fool.

No, he wasn't happy about what he'd discovered but he wasn't about to ignore it, either.

Leaning into the pouring rain, Lenore ducked into the day-care center's kitchen and shook her wet head. "It's dead."

Maggie wrung her hands. "What are we going to do?"

Shrugging out of the dripping yellow slicker, Lenore draped the garment over a chair and tiredly rubbed her face. This she did not need. As though she didn't have enough problems, it now seemed that the center's old yellow van had finally given up the ghost.

When Maggie persistently repeated her question, Lenore sighed. "We go to Plan B, that's all. Why don't you go read the kids a story or something? I'll handle the transportation."

"But it's pouring out there and school starts in less than an hour."

"I know." Lenore went to the wall phone, dialed quickly, then glanced over her shoulder at her worried assistant and offered a reassuring smile. "See to the children, Maggie. Everything will be fine."

The woman frowned but finally nodded and left the kitchen.

A familiar voice filtered through the lines. "Hello?"

"Hi, Grandma. Listen, can you put off your Meals-on-Wheels route for an hour or so?"

"Of course, dear. Is something wrong with the van again?"

"Yes. It won't start, just makes a funny clicking sound." Lenore flinched at a sudden crash from the dayroom. "I've got to go. See you in a few minutes."

Cradling the receiver, Lenore took a deep breath, rolled her eyes up in silent thanks, then dashed off to help poor Maggie.

Ten minutes later, two cars pulled up in front of the center. Lenore recognized Hettie's vintage pink sedan but the other vehicle, a sleek gray import, was unfamiliar. Her heart sank when Edison Collier stepped out. Did Hettie go anywhere without this man?

Before Lenore could build a healthy resentment, she was distracted by the line of excited children at the front door.

An exuberant eight-year-old muscled his way to Lenore's side. "Hey, Mrs. Blaine, are you gonna call my dad to fix that old van again?"

"Yes, Charlie, I'll call him just as soon as we get all o
you safely tucked into your classrooms."

"Dad likes to help out," Charlie said proudly. "He say
he owes you big time."

Lenore smiled. Charlie's dad was a single parent who ha
seen more than his share of rough times. Last year had bee
worse than most. The poor man's auto shop had gone belly
up and it had taken almost four months for him to fin
work. Lenore had waived the center's day-care fee durin
those months and in return, the man had been extremel
generous in sharing his considerable mechanical expertise
With the battered van on its last legs, Lenore had accepte
his offer more than once.

Some might have been too proud to take charity but Le
nore didn't see it that way. To her, life was a series of give
and-take situations. One shared what one could and some
how, generosity was always well rewarded.

Charlie's smiling face calmed Lenore and for the first tim
that morning, she felt assured that this, too, would pass. B
the time Hettie arrived on the front porch, Lenore was feel
ing more benevolent toward Edison, who was struggling t
aim an umbrella over Hettie's bouncing head and seeme
oblivious to the fact that he was personally soaked to th
skin.

Getting wet together was becoming a habit for those two
Lenore thought sourly. But she swallowed the memory o
last week's fiasco at her grandmother's apartment an
managed a stiff welcoming smile.

Once under the relative protection of the porch roo
Edison lowered the umbrella. He grinned at the gigglin
group pressed in the open doorway. "What beautiful chil
dren," he said to no one in particular. There was a softnes
in the old man's eyes, as though the mere sight of the chil
dren gave him great pleasure. That surprised Lenore. Sh
had always assumed that men like Edison—and Steven—
had remained bachelors because they had no use for eithe
children or commitment. But as Edison knelt to speak to
shy girl peeking around the doorway he certainly gave ever

appearance of being completely enamored of the youngsters.

She found herself wondering if Steven liked kids. Not that it really mattered, of course. She was just...wondering.

Hettie's bubbling voice broke into Lenore's daydream. "Let's see, dear, how many do we have today?"

"Umm? Oh, there's twelve."

"Gracious! Well, it's a good thing Sonny insisted on helping or we would've had to stack them like firewood." Hettie bent slightly and tickled a grinning towheaded boy as she continued her rapid-fire chatter. "Well we have three cars including yours, Lenore, so at four children apiece—" She straightened quickly and clapped her hands. "Perfect! Head 'em up and move 'em out," she chortled.

Edison chuckled and whipped up his trusty umbrella. Within a few minutes, each child had been escorted to a waiting vehicle and safely buckled inside. When the task was complete, Hettie slid into the driver's seat of her ancient car, stuck her head out the window and hollered, "Wagons ho!" as the miniature convoy rolled away.

A half hour later, Lenore had just ushered the last child into his classroom when the final bell rang. Exhausted, she leaned against the wall and stared down the corridor, waiting. Edison and Hettie had escorted the fourth-through-sixth graders to classrooms in the south wing of the sprawling elementary school, while Lenore had taken charge of the younger children.

In a moment, Hettie appeared. "My, those little ones are certainly exuberant."

Glancing past her grandmother, Lenore stared down the corridor. "Where's Edison?"

"Oh, he'll be along. This good-looking woman ran up and grabbed him like he was the last man on earth. Must be one of his ex-girlfriends." Hettie grinned and nudged Lenore knowingly. "A handsome old coot like that probably has a skeleton closet full of broken-hearted women."

Lenore was relieved by Hettie's cavalier attitude. After all, an emotionally attached woman wouldn't find the subject of a man's romantic escapades particularly amusing. Between Steven's suspicions and the jacuzzi incident, Lenore had been secretly worried. Those doubts obviously had no merit and she was massively relieved.

"Edison handles the children very well," Lenore said charitably.

"You sound surprised."

"I am," Lenore admitted. "I mean, he's never been married so I assumed he had no experience with children."

"Ah, now you know what I've always told you about assuming," Hettie said reproachfully. "Edison actually raised Steven, you know."

That was a shock. "Raised him? I don't understand."

"Such a tragedy, it was. Edison told me all about it. Why, after everything poor Steven suffered, it's a wonder he turned out to be such a fine man." Hettie gazed upward pitifully, shaking her head and making sad clicking sounds with her tongue. "Steven was only eight when it happened. It was a terrible thing."

The thought of Steven being subjected to some unknown horror jarred Lenore to her toes. "Good Lord, what happened?"

Hettie slid Lenore a sly look, then quickly turned away and sighed loudly. "Maybe I shouldn't say."

"Oh, for crying out loud, Grandma—"

"Well, if you insist." Hettie glanced quickly down the hallway, then lowered her voice. "Edison's brother—Steven's father—was an alcoholic. He wasn't a bad person, you understand, but he was weak. Anyway, the poor man couldn't hold a job and Steven's mother—Edison said she was a real shrew—was always threatening to take the boy and find a *real* man."

"How awful," Lenore murmured, trying to imagine how devastating it must have been for such a young child to be used as a pawn between parents.

Hettie regarded Lenore thoughtfully, judging the impact of her tale. With a satisfied nod, she continued. "When Steven was about eight, he suffered a terrible loss. Edison said that a friend of his committed suicide and the boy was absolutely shattered."

Lenore clutched her stomach. "My God, how horrible."

"But that wasn't the worst of it. Right after the funeral, Steven went home to find his parents fighting. Edison doesn't know the particulars, but apparently Steven's mother was screaming about being sick of living in poverty and then his father said that if he had to spend the rest of his life with an ungrateful wife and a kid who loved some crazy old wino more than his own father, he might as well jump off the building, too."

Lenore felt the blood drain from her face. "How could they have been that cruel?" she whispered as her hand absently touched her throat.

"They were probably so intent on hurting each other that they didn't even know he was there. Anyway, Steven packed his little bag and ran away. Edison said that his parents were searching for him when their car crashed. They were killed instantly."

Lenore turned away, sickened by the image her grandmother's words evoked. To such a little boy, the combination of tragedies must have been devastating. She could imagine the inconsolable guilt and feelings of abandonment. Her heart went out to the child and ached for the solitary man he had become.

Hettie was watching Lenore closely, gauging her horrified expression before adding, "Edison took the boy in and raised him, and a darned good job he did, too. Steven's a fine and decent man . . . a little moody, maybe, but being a Cancer he really can't help that. It's the moon, you know."

"Yes, I know," Lenore murmured absently, her mind still engrossed in the disturbing images Hettie's story had evoked. The thought of Steven being subjected to such mental torment bothered Lenore more than she would have imagined possible. After all, she barely knew Steven Collier.

Well, that wasn't completely true. She hadn't known him for long but felt an intuitive kinship with him. They were connected somehow and Lenore was drawn to Steven on a level she didn't quite understand. That bothered her, as did the random invasion of her mind, the unwanted images of

Steven's angular features and brooding eyes that filtered into her thoughts at the most inopportune moments.

Even more distressing was the way Lenore felt during these transitory moments. She became restless and fidgety, her skin warming to the point of discomfort. And there was this peculiar ache, an insatiable hunger that confused and frightened her. Even now while she rationally attempted to analyze these feelings, a slow heat was rising from deep inside.

Exhaling, Lenore squeezed her eyelids shut and shook her head in disgust. This was ridiculous. She was a grown woman, not an adolescent in the throes of raging hormones. Steven Collier was no different than any other man.

In spite of the stern mental rebuke, a secret part of Lenore recognized the evasion of her flinching heart. Steven Collier was special. Deep down, Lenore knew that and it scared her half to death.

Hettie's voice broke into Lenore's reverie. "Yoo-hoo! Sonny!"

Blinking, Lenore took a moment to recall that she was still standing at the elementary school before following Hettie's excited wave. Looking down the corridor, Lenore saw Edison sauntering toward them and beside him was a trim, well-dressed woman. When they were close, Lenore recognized the woman as the school principal, Eleanor Briggs.

"You must be Hettie," Mrs. Briggs said warmly. "Edison has been telling me all about you."

Edison beamed as Hettie playfully swatted his arm. "Don't you believe any of it. The man is an incorrigible liar."

Mrs. Briggs laughed and nodded knowingly, then turned to Lenore. "It's so nice to see you again, Lenore. I understand the center's van is having problems again. Nothing serious, I hope."

"I doubt it," Lenore replied lightly. "I think the old rust bucket has an aversion to rain. Every time the sky clouds up, it simply refuses to budge."

Edison found that amusing. "The dampness probably makes its gears ache. My old bones can relate to that."

Mrs. Briggs laughed. "Now, Ed, you've always said that a good man, like fine wine, always improves with age."

Hettie emitted a disbelieving snort but her little eyes sparkled. "More like aged cheese, I'd say, moldy around the edges but still fresh and firm where it counts."

Edison actually blushed. Shuffling uncomfortably, he muttered, "We'd, uh, best be getting back."

Glancing at her watch, Hettie made a soft tsking sound. "Oh, my, yes. Lunch deliveries start in an hour."

With that pronouncement, Hettie gave Lenore a quick hug then snagged Edison's wrist and, waving happily over her shoulder, she hauled the big man away.

When they had left, Mrs. Briggs was still smiling. "They make a cute couple."

Lenore's head snapped around. "They're not a couple," she said with a bit too much emphasis. "They're simply friends."

The principal's smile faded. "I'm sorry to hear that."

"Pardon me?"

"I've never seen Edison so animated. He just seemed so happy I naturally assumed..." The words evaporated and Mrs. Briggs shrugged.

Lenore regarded the woman. "I didn't realize that you and Mr. Collier were acquainted."

"Edison made it his business to be acquainted with as many people as possible. Before he retired, he was one of the most influential men in the county. I met him during his tenure on the school board."

"Edison Collier was on the school board?"

"Yes, for over eight years. He was quite good, too. I was disappointed that he decided not to run for a third term." Mrs. Briggs regarded Lenore thoughtfully. "Actually I was a bit suspicious at first. I didn't think that a bachelor would have a substantive interest in our children's education, particularly in light of Edison's reputation but as it turned out—"

"Reputation?" Lenore interrupted, instantly alert. "What reputation?"

Mrs. Briggs cocked her head. "You don't know, do you?"

"No, no, I don't."

The principal glanced down the deserted corridor. "This is just rumor, you understand, but I have it on rather good authority that in his prime Edison was considered, well, quite a ladies' man."

It was all Lenore could do to keep from shaking the poor woman but she managed a calm demeanor. "Oh, really?"

"Yes, indeed. Over the years, Edison held several prominent positions so his presence at various social and political functions was always in demand. He attended with a variety of lovely young women, but was rarely seen with the same one twice so naturally tongues would wag." With another glance to assure she wouldn't be overheard, Mrs. Briggs lowered her voice to a conspiratorial whisper. "He broke a lot of hearts, that one. Why, I once heard that a woman was so distraught when he stopped seeing her that she climbed on to a freeway overpass and threatened to jump. Of course, that was a long time ago."

Lenore was speechless. Nagging doubt erupted into full-fledged suspicion, but she didn't believe Hettie could be victimized by the dubious lure of an aging Lothario any more than she herself could be.

Then Lenore thought of Steven's smoldering intensity and her heart twisted. If Hettie's emotions were as fallible as her own, perhaps they were both doomed.

Chapter Five

Lenore collapsed on the sofa and glanced at her watch. She still had a couple of hours before her regular Wednesday dinner date with Hettie and was grateful for the opportunity to catch up on some household chores. The past two days had been punishing but things were finally looking up. Charlie's dad had repaired the recalcitrant van, yesterday's rainstorm had finally moved east and she'd actually found a bank that was willing to consider a third mortgage on her canyon home.

Even Lenore's distress at discovering Edison's notorious past had been put into perspective. After all, that had been years ago and in spite of occasional lapses, Lenore had to admit that she secretly liked Edison. He'd been so good with the children and had radiated a warmth and sincerity that simply couldn't have been faked.

Besides, a man who'd given such a loving home to a traumatized child certainly couldn't be all bad. Clearly the old goat had some redeeming characteristics and although Mrs. Briggs's revelations had been initially startling, Lenore had eventually concluded that good looks weren't a crime. It certainly hadn't been the poor man's fault that women had once found him attractive.

Lenore had no doubt that in his day, Edison had been a hunky devil because Steven and his uncle bore an incredibly strong family resemblance. In fact, if he'd been half as appealing as his nephew, she could certainly understand why women had flocked to him like moths to a flame.

Some women, that is. Certainly not her grandmother. In spite of her recent lapse in confidence, Lenore remained deeply convinced that Hettie was also immune to the masculine mystique. Only one love was allotted per lifetime and be it curse or blessing, both woman had used their quota.

As Lenore silently argued that there was nothing romantic between Hettie and Edison, she noticed that her answering machine was blinking. Absently she wandered over to retrieve her messages.

Beep. "Hi, Lenore. This is Martha Winger. Just wanted to let you know that Heather won't be going to class tomorrow. I'm sure it's nothing serious, but she, um, has this little rash. I'll let you know what the doctor says."

Lenore winced. Rashes made her nervous. Last year, chicken pox had temporarily felled forty percent of the center's population. Another epidemic like that would propel The Happy Lamb into instant insolvency.

Beep. "This is Charlie's dad. Say, did I leave a set of socket wrenches in the van? Give me a call..."

As the various voices droned from the tape, Lenore glanced through the French doors and admired the greening garden. Spring weather had sent some of the plants into a growing frenzy and she mentally made a note to pick up some plant food this weekend.

Beep. "Lenore...can you hear me, child?" The last part of Hettie's sentence was distorted by a deafening roar. "Oh, these newfangled jet planes are so noisy a body can't hear themselves think."

Lenore's head snapped around and she stared at the whirring machine. "Grandma?"

The taped din decreased and Lenore heard her grandmother's unmistakable chuckle. "There, that's better. Listen, dear, I'm going to have to cancel our dinner tonight...could you feed Buster for a few days? You have a key, don't you? Oh, of course you do. Anyway, I'm at the airport. Sonny had the most exciting surprise...you'll never guess!'' Hettie paused as another engine screamed, then continued breathlessly. ''Gracious, I'm so excited. We're flying to Miami. Sonny booked us on a cruise ship and...are you ready for this...he's taking me to the Bahamas! Can you imagine? *The Bahamas!* Oh, I know this is quite sudden, dear, but we were looking at one of those travel magazines at the doctor's office—Sonny takes allergy shots, you know—and there were these romantic pictures of white sand and blue water. Well, I'd never seen anything so beautiful and next thing I know, Sonny's telling me to pack a bag. Isn't he wonderful? Anyway, we'll be back sometime Sunday. I'll call you then. Don't forget about Buster, dear.''

There was a brief pause, then a click and a dial tone.

Dazed, Lenore simply stared at the stupid machine. A romantic cruise to the Bahamas? Her stomach tightened into a hard ball as her deepest fears about Edison Collier were suddenly confirmed. The old geezer was out to seduce her vulnerable grandmother.

''Look here, Chester, that bedrock should have been blasted three days ago.'' It wasn't easy to maintain a calm tone when each day's delay cost thousands, but somehow Steven managed to be rational in the face of his latest financial disaster.

The ragged crew chief shrugged nonchalantly and scratched his whiskered chin. ''Yep.''

Steven swallowed a furious reply. The man's indolent attitude could make a nun cuss. Blood pressure rising, Steven angrily gestured toward the work site where a group of men lounged idly. ''I've got an entire foundation crew on standby. What the hell are you waiting for, divine intervention?''

The squat little man squinted up. ''Caps.''

''Caps? You mean blasting caps?''

Chester spit noisily and wiped his mouth on his forearm. "Yep."

Steven took a deep breath, folded his arms and stared down at his steel-toed boots. He had to stay calm, to maintain control of this infuriating situation. Finally he gave the man a hard look and spoke through clenched teeth. "And just when, pray tell, will these elusive caps be on site?"

"Just got here." The chief jerked his dirty thumb toward a group of workers unloading cargo from a transport vehicle. "Soon as we get them charges set, we'll blow that rock outta there faster than a flea can bite yer dog's butt."

Irritation turned to instant relief. Steven's breath slid out slowly and he issued silent thanks that at least one of his problems was near resolution. "Good," Steven mumbled, lifting his hard hat to wipe his damp forehead. "With a little luck, the parking structure will be back on schedule within a couple weeks."

With an indifferent nod, Chester eyed the gaping hole that would become the structure's basement, then spit on a rock and sauntered toward his crew. "Hustle, boys. Boss man is gettin' his shorts in a twist again."

With a long-suffering sigh, Steven rolled his eyes up and gazed heavenward. "Why me?" he mumbled. If Chester hadn't been the best in the business, Steven would have already kicked his obnoxious tail all the way back to the union hall—

"Mr. Collier!"

Shading his eyes, Steven looked toward the trailer that served as his office and saw his secretary waving from the tiny porch.

The woman cupped her mouth and hollered over the construction din. "You have a call. I think it's important."

Steven hesitated, reluctant to leave the site at such a crucial moment. Still, his secretary was top-notch and if she said the call was important, then it damn well *was* important.

Glancing over his shoulder, he saw the final box of blasting caps had been opened and were in the process of being counted. If the call didn't take long, he should be back before they started the charges.

Decision made, he picked his way down the steel scaffolding and met his secretary at the trailer.

"It's Jonas Berringer," she told him somberly.

Steven paused in midstride. "Edison's stockbroker?"

"Yes." She chewed her lip nervously. "He seemed, well, concerned."

As usual, Steven's first thought was of potential disaster. The biggest chunk of Edison's retirement income was derived from stock dividends and mutual funds. If Berringer's impeccably accurate grapevine was predicting a major decline in the market, Edison's financial security could be jeopardized.

With a mumbled "Thank you," Steven strode to his office and closed the door. He took a deep breath and lifted the receiver. "What's happening, Jonas? Has the market taken a nosedive?"

"Not at all," came the tense reply. "What remains of your uncle's portfolio is quite sound."

Steven's knees buckled and he fell back into his chair. "What . . . the hell does that mean?"

"It means simply that in the past twenty-four hours, your uncle has sold off nearly eleven percent of his holdings."

Head spinning, Steven braced his elbows on the desk and tried to gather his thoughts. "There must be some mistake."

"That's exactly what I thought when the sell order was received. I called Edison personally for verification." Berringer's voice softened. "There was no mistake, Steven."

Bewildered, Steven tried to mentally formulate a reason that made sense. His uncle was usually as sharp as a tack when it came to financial matters. "Maybe Edison decided to diversify, reinvest those funds in long-term bonds or something."

After a brief pause, Berringer dashed any such hope. "I questioned him on that, assuming that if he had such plans, perhaps I could counsel him on the specifics."

"What did he say?"

Berringer cleared his throat. "Only that he wanted cash for, er, fun money."

"*Fun money?*" Steven was certain he'd misheard.

No such luck. Berringer confirmed the terminology, then added, "Apparently Edison and a friend were planning a trip—to the Bahamas, I believe—and something was mentioned about donating funds to Active Seniors for Political Reform."

The blood drained from Steven's face. "This...friend. Did he mention a name?"

"No, not that I recall." Berringer paused. "I've spent most of the day considering whether or not to call you on this matter—"

"You did the right thing, Jonas. I appreciate your concern." Steven pinched the bridge of his nose, as though the gesture could exorcise the sudden pain shooting through his skull. Establishing the identity of Edison's "friend" was merely a formality.

Steven felt positively ill as his worst fears were undeniably confirmed. Sweet-faced, apple-cheeked Hester Gregory was nothing more than a gold digger.

If Hettie was a fraud, so was Lenore. And that was devastating.

Stumbling over a discarded scrap of steel, Lenore steadied herself then scanned the construction site searching for Steven. He had to stop this madness. She didn't know how he could manage that neat trick but rational thought dissipated the moment she'd received her grandmother's shocking message. Lenore's immediate reaction had been that Steven would know what to do. Later she'd analyze the implications of that overwhelming urge; now, she was simply running on instinct.

It was late afternoon, damp and dismal, with a wet blanket of fog lurking off the coast. The weather matched Lenore's mood as she struggled across the muddy, rock-strewn construction area wishing she'd had the foresight to exchange high heels for more sensible footwear.

There was no time to worry about that now. She had to find Steven and stopped again to visually search the area. Except for a small group of men working in a deep excavation, the site seemed nearly deserted. Beside the huge pit, an iron-and-steel skeleton rose like a giant carcass, its girdered bones casting eerie shadows over the scarred land.

A disquieting sense of uneasiness settled over Lenore, a déjà vu of another time and place. The crisscrossing iron beams reminded her of something else—something ominous that she didn't want to remember. A lump of fear lodged in her throat, followed by the metallic taste of mounting panic.

An image flashed through her mind, a vision of sprawling steel scaffolds and a towering tangle of iron pipes silhouetted against a blood-red sky.

The refinery.

Lenore squeezed her eyes closed, shaking her head as though the movement could throw out the unwanted memory, but the horrible image remained. It was so real that Lenore actually relived that long-ago moment and felt the scalding wind sear her lungs. In her mind she heard the thunderous eruption that had split the quiet night as though hell itself had exploded.

Lenore recalled running to the tiny balcony of their apartment and stared in horror at the glowing sky. She'd known instantly what had happened.

Oh, dear God.

Her fingers had gripped the rail so tightly that her nails cut into her palms but she'd been too horrified to move. Everything had seemed surrealistic, dreamlike. Paralyzed, Lenore had watched in morbid fascination as thick smoke spiraled upward, partially obscuring the crimson flame licking the black horizon.

She was transported into her worst nightmare, stalked by an unseen horror yet rooted to the ground as the terror came closer and closer. Muted by fear, her mouth contorted in a soundless scream.

This couldn't be real. Please, Lord, this can't be happening.

The mournful wail of distant sirens echoed through the blackness like the terrified cries of a thousand dying souls. And she knew then that it was real, hideously real.

As Lenore watched helplessly, thunderheads of smoke exploded upward, smothering the moon and choking the land with an acrid stench of burned oil and vaporized flesh. That night changed Lenore's life forever. Gone was the innocence of youth, the joy of life. She saw purgatory. She smelled death. She was alone.

"Hey, lady! Look out!"

The sharp warning broke into Lenore's reverie. Dazed, she glanced toward the source of sound and saw a squat, beefy man wearing a yellow helmet and waving wildly. Lenore looked down and froze. She was less than a foot from the edge of the yawning pit. In another moment, she would have blithely plunged over the edge. The realization turned her skin to ice and she feebly stumbled backward.

Before she could so much as stammer a "thank you," the construction worker grunted in disgust. "Watch where you're goin', lady. This ain't no shopping mall."

Lenore simply nodded, too shaken to be offended. She licked her lips and clasped her hands together in a vain attempt to stop them from trembling. But it wasn't the close call causing her violent physical reaction; it was the memories.

She took a deep breath and managed a stiff smile. "Can you tell me where to find Steven Collier?"

The man scowled, jerked his thumb toward a small silver trailer on the far side of the site, then hoisted a carton to his shoulder and descended a ladder down onto the excavation floor.

Lungs aching, Lenore realized that she'd been holding her breath and exhaled slowly. She turned, willed her knees not to buckle and walked stiffly toward the trailer. When she was less than fifty feet away, the door flew open.

Steven burst out, hollering over his shoulder to someone still inside the tiny office. "Keep dialing. If you reach my uncle, tell him to wait for me. I'll be there in fifteen minutes."

Whirling, he strode quickly down the steps and lurched to a stop directly in front of Lenore. His eyes widened.

"Edison's gone," Lenore announced brusquely, then folded her arms and gave him a killing stare. "Your uncle is on his way to Miami with my grandmother."

Steven's eyes reflected in genuine shock before narrowing dangerously. A tiny muscle on the curve of his jaw twitched and Lenore noted with some interest that his entire body had visibly tensed.

From his stunned reaction, Lenore judged that Steven hadn't been party to his uncle's nefarious plan. She was relieved, although not surprised. Lenore didn't fully understand why Steven was annoyed by Hettie and Edison's relationship but his disapproval made him an ally. For that she was grateful.

Steven regarded her with quiet intensity. "So, are you here to gloat?"

Stunned, Lenore stumbled back as though she'd been pushed. "I beg your pardon?"

"I wouldn't have thought that your style," he replied tightly. "But we really don't know each other very well, do we?"

Totally bewildered by this unexpected response, Lenore pushed her bangs out of her eyes and stared at him in confusion. "What in the world are you talking about?"

Tipping back his hard hat, Steven slowly gazed the length of her body with an insolence that made her shudder. "You may have won the first battle, but I've got news for you, honey. The war has just begun."

Lenore was ticked off by his impudence and felt her own anger rising. "If you're not having a delayed reaction to having been beaned at the ball game, then that funny plastic bowl on your head must be too tight because you're not making one darn bit of sense."

Steven simply eyed her coldly. "You can stop the righteous indignation act anytime. I know what's going on."

"You do?" She was instantly deflated. "And you're just going to let it happen?"

"Of course not," he snapped.

"Thank God." She wondered why he was staring incredulously but she didn't care if the man was cross-eyed and drooling as long as he kept his uncle from breaking poor Hettie's heart.

After a moment, Steven jammed his hands into his pockets, rocked back on his heels and spoke quietly. "I know how desperately your day-care center needs money and I'll even try to help you if I can, but I won't allow my uncle to be exploited as a meal ticket."

Lenore didn't quite believe what she was hearing. "The only person being exploited here is my grandma— Wait a minute. What has the day-care center got to do with any of this?"

He shrugged. "It's nearly bankrupt."

"How do you know that?" Before the words were out, Lenore knew the answer and was infuriated. "You've been spying on me, haven't you?"

"Some background investigation seemed prudent."

"Why you pompous, arrogant..." Words failed her and after a sputtering moment, she blasted him again. "*How dare you?* What gives you the right to pry into my personal life, sneaking around, skulking in shadows like some slimy voyeur—"

Angrily Steven interrupted her. "I have every right to do whatever it takes to protect my uncle."

"Protect him from what?" Interpreting his sullen glare, Lenore pressed her palm against her own chest and nearly laughed in amazement. "Were you expecting my four-foot-eleven-inch grandmother to mug your six-foot uncle right there in the complex lobby? Or did you suspect a conspiracy? Well, you caught us, bozo. Granny and I had it all planned. She was going to wrestle him to the ground so I could empty his pockets. Then we were going to handcuff him to a light pole and skip town until the heat was off, see? Actually we're on the lam now from a bank job in Peoria."

Steven emitted a sound of utter disgust. "There's nothing funny about this."

"I agree." Feet planted, hands on hips, Lenore lifted her chin in challenge. "So what are you going to do about it?"

"For one thing, I'm going to make certain my uncle doesn't end up in a soup kitchen."

Taken aback, Lenore murmured, "I didn't know that Edison was having financial problems."

"He wasn't, until your grandmother came along." Steven pursed his lips. "Are you saying that you didn't know my uncle cashed in part of his retirement fund to finance this little jaunt?"

"Of course not." Lenore's expression mirrored her shock. "That's why you've been making all these insulting insinuations?"

Steven shifted uncomfortably and absently rubbed his neck. "Edison told his broker that he had some friends that needed help. I naturally assumed..." His voice trailed away and he gazed awkwardly into space.

"You assumed wrong," Lenore snapped. "Do you actually believe I go around begging money from people I hardly know?"

"No, but since Hettie co-owns the center, it wasn't unreasonable to consider that she might have, ah, requested a loan."

"You really have been checking up on us, haven't you?" Without awaiting an answer, Lenore flicked her hand as though shooing a fly. "It's none of your business, but since you insist on butting into my affairs, you might as well get it right. My grandmother has nothing to do with the operation of the center. Her initial investment has been paid back with interest and she's still listed as a co-owner because I want it that way. The center does have, um, a minor cash-flow problem at the moment but Grandma doesn't know anything about it."

"Why not?" Steven frowned skeptically.

"The situation is temporary and I'm dealing with it." Uncomfortable with the focus of conversation, she shifted the subject. "Anyway I don't understand why you're suddenly so concerned about Edison's checkbook. Your uncle didn't build an entire development corporation from the ground up by being a fiscal idiot. Obviously he is an intelligent man."

"He's also an extremely generous man, which makes him susceptible to the greedy and unscrupulous."

"Oh, well, thank you very much."

"I didn't mean to imply— Oh, hell." Turning away, Steven took a shuddering breath and stared at the ground, but not before Lenore had seen the pain in his eyes and realized just how devoted Steven was to his uncle. She admired that. And she understood it.

"You really are worried about Edison, aren't you?" she asked softly.

He tried a nonchalant shrug that didn't quite cover the emotion in his voice. "I don't want to see him end up in the gutter, that's all."

"Why would you believe that could happen?"

"I've seen it happen," Steven said with a bitterness that shocked Lenore to the core. "Good men thrown into society's scrap heap because they're old and worn-out are prime prey for any flimflam artist offering a way to regain their self-esteem. In the end, they wind up victimized and disillusioned, convinced that society was right. Their lives are worthless." He closed his eyes and took a ragged breath, his angular features creased in an expression of pure torment, as though he was reliving some past horror.

Lenore could hardly breathe, recalling what Hettie had confided about Steven's tormented youth. The scenario Steven had related with such emotion and pain was not, Lenore suspected, an impersonal generic anecdote. Whether he'd intended to or not, Steven had offered a glimpse of his soul and in doing so, had given Lenore remarkable insight into his paladin personality.

Annoyance at having her privacy violated quickly dissolved into compassion. She understood him now. There was nothing he wouldn't do to protect the one stable person in his life.

That was something they had in common.

Because Lenore couldn't think of any other way to comfort him, she simply laid a reassuring hand on his arm. "If I had your connections, I probably would have compiled a dossier on you, too."

He looked down at the slim hand resting on his forearm then raised his gaze to her face, scrutinizing her so fiercely that she shivered. Lord he was handsome. No wonder he was still a bachelor. Women probably fell at his feet, hoping he'd favor them with an interested glance. Those penetrating green eyes were intimidating, seeming to peel away her protective veneer and expose the secret fantasies lurking deep inside. It was frightening. It was exciting.

It was dangerous.

Breaking the visual stalemate, Lenore turned away and knotted her trembling hands together. She tested her voice. "So, I'm sure you can understand why I'm so concerned about my grandmother."

"Just what exactly are you concerned about?"

"I think that's fairly obvious." Lenore's face heated. "There is this cruise thing, after all."

"Hmm. And you suspect that they'll be, well, sharing more than a cabin?"

"Certainly not! I've told you that my grandmother is not in the market for romantic entanglements."

Steven was fascinated by the red flush staining Lenore's soft throat and the way she fanned herself with her hand. She was embarrassed and he found that oddly charming. But he was still somewhat puzzled and said so.

She fiddled with a loose button on her linen suit jacket. "My grandmother is rather vulnerable when it comes to men."

"Vulnerable? Hettie?" Steven chuckled. "I've seen armored tanks more vulnerable than your grandmother. Besides, when I brought this up last week you scoffed at the notion and told me that she would always be faithful to your grandfather's memory."

"That's absolutely true," Lenore insisted, nodding vigorously. Then her voice softened, taking on a dreamy quality. "Grandpa is the only man she has ever loved. Even though he has been gone for nearly ten years, Grandma still wears his wedding ring."

Silently Steven reached down and lifted her left hand. He delicately caressed her bare fingers, silently questioning.

Then a strange thing happened. Lenore stared dumbly at her own hand, eyes glazed as though her mind had traveled to some distant plane. As Steven watched in fascination, she frowned slightly and he saw a flash of white as she absently nibbled her lower lip. Suddenly her eyes widened in horror. Pulling away from him, she clasped her hands together and pressed them against her heart. She was trembling and Steven reached out, succumbing to an overwhelming urge to hold her.

Instantly she stepped back, catching one high heel on a rock and lurching awkwardly. He caught her shoulders, steadying her as he studied her lucid expression. Where ever she had mentally traveled, she was back now.

"Are you all right?"

"Yes, thank you." She offered a strained smile as proof. "Now, about my grandmother. I don't think this, ah, friendship with Edison is good for her. Emotionally that is."

Something had clearly upset Lenore, but apparently she didn't want to discuss it so Steven respected her silent request and returned to the subject at hand. "Even if my uncle did make a pass at Hettie, she'd just turn him down flat, right?"

To his surprise, she hesitated. "I . . . suppose so." When he hiked one eyebrow, Lenore flushed to the roots of her shiny sable hair and stammered an explanation. "I mean, my grandmother is only human. She isn't particularly experienced with men, on a romantic level of course, and well, she's been alone a long time . . ." Her voice trailed away and she extended her hand in a helpless gesture that tugged at Steven's heart.

There was sadness in her voice that had a surprisingly potent effect on him. That bothered him, so he shifted restlessly and made a production of rolling down the sleeves of his plaid work shirt. "So why do you feel that Hettie might be susceptible to the lure of moonlight and soft music?"

Then he looked at her. That was a mistake. Their eyes locked and at that moment, Steven lost track of where he was and who he was, totally absorbed in the power of her luminous gaze.

She moistened her lips with her tongue and swallowed hard, never breaking their visual stalemate. When she spoke, her voice had a soft, ethereal quality. "Loneliness is a bleak companion. Sometimes at night the ache begins, an emptiness that screams out for fulfillment. There's this incredible longing to see desire in a man's eyes and feel the heat of his passion . . . to be cherished again . . . and to be loved."

Steven's mouth went dry and a shiver traveled the length of him from nape to spine. Lenore wasn't intoning textbook psychology here. Unconsciously or not, she had just described with stunning power the depth of her own visceral desire. The realization took his breath away.

For that brief moment, he felt as though their souls had touched and he was dizzy with the power of that union. He wanted to speak, but couldn't. He wanted to reach out, but was paralyzed. He wanted her and she knew it.

When he pulled her close, she didn't resist. Her lips parted in welcome and he accepted the tender invitation. She tasted as sweet as he'd dreamed but her response was beyond his wildest imagination. She moaned low in her throat and the sensuous sound nearly drove him crazy. He deepened the kiss and tightened his grip, his mind swirling with brilliant flashes of vivid light.

There really were fireworks, he thought fuzzily, just as the romance novels predicted. He wondered if the earth would move, too.

Vaguely Steven recognized the distant call. "Fire in the hole!" In the deepest recess of his mind, a warning light glowed but he was too mesmerized to react quickly enough.

The explosion shook the ground like a mortar blast.

Chapter Six

The concussion knocked Lenore backward and as Steven extended a steadying hand, she pushed violently away, gasping. Hands flailing wildly, her terrified gaze was locked on the plume of dust rising from the excavation pit.

"It's the blasters," Steven explained, unnerved by her violent reaction. "Everything's under control."

She clutched her throat, eyes darting like a trapped animal. "I...have to go." She pushed by him and stumbled toward the parking area.

After a stunned moment, Steven followed and took hold of her arm. "What's wrong?"

"Nothing," she replied raggedly. "Nothing at all. I'll call you tomorrow. We'll talk."

Reluctantly Steven released her and watched as she hurried across the muddy terrain. He was confused by her panicked reaction. She hadn't simply been startled by an unexpected noise; she'd been absolutely horrified. That bothered him immensely and his own compelling need to offer comfort was just as distressing.

The woman had gotten to Steven and he didn't like that one bit.

While he was mentally sorting through these bizarre events, Lenore had progressed down the rocky slope toward her car. As she passed several construction workers, one of the men called out. Lenore stopped, waiting as the man worked his way over the debris. The grinning man greeted Lenore enthusiastically and shook her hand so vigorously, Steven was afraid that her poor arm might break off at the shoulder. After a brief conversation, Lenore left and the worker returned to his duties.

The odd scene piqued Steven's curiosity and he quickly strode over to check the situation out. The worker who'd stopped Lenore was busily repacking unused blasting caps when he saw Steven. The poor fellow snapped to attention, his Adam's apple bobbing furiously. "Mr. Collier, sir," he stammered, before words failed him completely.

Steven got right to the point. "You're new, aren't you?"

"Yes, sir, I am. Started last week. This is a great job, though . . . best I ever had. I'm truly grateful to you for the opportunity, sir." Wringing his hands, the man shifted quickly from one foot to the other.

Ordinarily Steven would have recognized and alleviated the worker's obvious fear of an approaching reprimand, but at the moment Steven's mind wasn't on the crewman's distress. "That woman you were just speaking to, do you know her?"

"Mrs. Blaine? Why, yes, sir, I do." He spread his hands deferentially. "She watches my kids for me. Salt of the earth, that woman. Wouldn't know what I'd have done these past months without her."

"What do you mean by that?" Steven demanded.

Stiffening, the man teetered back. "She, uh, helped us out through some hard times, that's all."

"In what way?" Steven realized he sounded like a drill sergeant but he couldn't quite help himself. This guy had information about Lenore. Steven wanted that information and he wanted it now.

The worker wiped his sweaty forehead. "I, uh, was out of work for a while. Mrs. Blaine didn't hassle me for money, just said that she'd take care of the kids until I got back on my feet. Now that I'm working steady . . ." He paused here, as though awaiting confirmation. Steven nodded brusquely and the man was visibly relieved. "Anyway, I was telling her that I'd be paying double now, till we're caught up."

Steven frowned, rubbed his chin and tried to digest that interesting tidbit of information. Such generosity didn't seem consistent with the behavior of a money-grubbing woman, particularly since the day-care center was in such dire financial straits.

Although wariness was an intrinsic part of Steven's nature, so was the ability to reevaluate theories when new information was available. If he'd been wrong about Lenore's motives, it was possible that he'd also been wrong about Hettie's.

The only way to sort out such contradictory evidence was through intensive observation. And he was rather looking forward to that.

Somehow Lenore managed to negotiate the winding road home without careening off a cliff. By the time she turned into her steep driveway, her fingers ached from their death grip on the steering wheel. Still shaking, she flipped off the ignition. With a ragged sob, she buried her face in her arms, collapsed against the wheel and wept.

The explosion had initiated a terrifying flashback of the night Michael had died but Lenore had relived that night a thousand times before. This time, something had been different. There had been a new memory, still vague yet so horrifying that she had instantly blocked out the image and had been overwhelmed by uncontrollable hysteria.

Part of Lenore wanted to ignore what had happened, to suppress the sickening fear of recalling what was too painful to endure. But her ingrained sense of logic intruded, insisting that whatever lurked in the black part of her mind couldn't be expelled without first being understood. So she suppressed a wave of nausea, bit her lip until she tasted blood, and concentrated on the events leading up to her panic attack.

She'd been uncomfortable at the site but had managed at least a modicum of control—until the explosion.

That deafening blast had been the catalyst, but as she thought back, she realized that even before the detonation there had been other warning signals, particularly when she'd realized that Steven was going to kiss her. And she'd wanted that, drawn by some inexplicable need and a desire that went well beyond the realm of idle curiosity.

Apparently her attraction to Steven Collier went deeper than she'd first realized. In spite of her conscious denial, her pulse raced oddly in his presence and a peculiar heat spiraled up from the secret part of her that had been dormant so long. Even as Steven had gently pulled her close, his lips parted and eyes questioning, alarms had echoed through her passion-fogged mind. So desperate was her need that she'd ignored the warnings, craving only the solace of his embrace and the tender touch of his warm mouth.

Now Lenore remembered that sweet moment and something odd happened. Disjointed images flashed through her mind, images of Michael's face, angry and contorted.

Squeezing her eyes closed, she straightened and rubbed her lids with icy palms. Guilt stabbed her like a steel blade and she was overwhelmed by a sense of betrayal so acute that she nearly cried.

Yet the emotional upheaval made no sense. Michael hadn't been the jealous type and Lenore intuitively knew that her fervid feelings didn't stem from simply being attracted to another man. These were reflexive reactions to ghost images from the past.

As Lenore struggled with the confusing and contradictory recollections, she absently massaged her left hand as Steven had done.

The ring.

Lenore wore no wedding ring and Steven had silently questioned that. It had been a question she couldn't answer because she couldn't remember. On the day of Michael's funeral, she recalled searching frantically for the lovely etched band. Eventually she'd bitterly realized that the cherished ring had been lost, probably when she'd fought through the police line into the frenzied turmoil outside the flaming refinery.

Now she held her hand up, scrutinizing her bare fingers in the waning light of the setting sun. She stared until her eyes burned and she could barely focus. Then her hand blurred and metamorphosed. Her short, blunt-cut fingernails were suddenly lithe and long, professionally manicured and lacquered with the shiny red polish she'd favored years ago.

And on her third finger, gleamed the intricate gold wedding band that had been in Michael's family for years. Transported back in time, Lenore turned her hand, admiring how the diamond-cut pattern sparkled in even the palest light. In the sudden flood of memories, she even recalled how worried Michael had been that she wouldn't be pleased with a "used" wedding band.

But Lenore had cherished the ring and its history. It had been part of Michael and so she had loved it as she had loved him. She'd never taken it off. Never.

Except...

A sense of uneasiness fell over her. She squirmed nervously, unwilling to blink lest she break the fragile link with this elusive part of her past. As she continued to stare at the phantom ring, her mind swirled back through the years until a vision formed with startling clarity.

She remembered. Dear God, she remembered.

Michael had been angry. He seemed to be shouting but the recollection carried no sound. As though Lenore were a detached observer from another dimension, she studied the visualization and realized that Michael had been shouting at her. They'd been arguing about something.

That was odd, she thought absently. Consciously she'd never recalled a serious disagreement with Michael yet the memories continued surging forward. This *had* happened, but why? And why had she not remembered before now?

Suddenly she envisioned the argument growing more bitter. Then, like a scene from some trite B-movie, Lenore recalled removing the wedding band and dramatically hurling it across the room.

Angrily Michael had retrieved the ring. Lenore had said something—she couldn't remember what—then Michael had dropped the ring into his pocket and stalked out the door.

Lenore had never seen Michael or the ring again.

With a ragged gasp, Lenore tried to suppress the mental deluge but it was too late. The amnesiac numbness had dissipated and she remembered it all.

She remembered the day she'd mischievously emptied her ice cream cone in Michael's shorts and how he'd laughingly retaliated by nudging her into a nearby fountain.

She remembered the hours they'd spent worrying about bills and daydreaming about their future children.

She remembered Michael's lazy smile and how he would sulk if he didn't get his own way.

She remembered it all, the good and the bad, the joys and the sorrows.

And she remembered that had it not been for her, Michael would still be alive.

Lenore was pruning shrubbery when Steven drove up. Her mouth went dry at the sight of him and the involuntary reaction annoyed her immensely. By the time he'd climbed the steep walk to her front door, she was guarded and irritable.

As usual he was dressed like a salvage-yard reject, wearing frayed jeans and a loose upper garment that might have been a sleeveless sweatshirt. If the clothing was shapeless, the body was not. No amount of torn fleece could conceal his muscular shoulders or disguise biceps honed by years of physical labor.

If Edison in his prime had even remotely resembled his stunning nephew, Lenore could understand and empathize with the broken hearts he'd left in his wake.

But despite understandable temptation, Lenore was determined that neither she nor her grandmother would add another notch to a Collier bachelor belt.

Thus mentally reinforced, Lenore dropped her pruning shears and casually brushed her hands together as she stood. As was her habit when nervous, she talked a blue streak without allowing time for response. "You made good time. Did you have any trouble finding the place? This canyon can be a little tricky if you're not familiar with it. Warm today, isn't it? Perhaps we should go inside. I don't have air-conditioning but it's still cooler...would you like something to drink?"

By the time she paused, her hand was on the doorknob and she glanced over her shoulder. Steven declined her offer of refreshment and staunchly followed her inside.

Dropping her gloves on the entry table, Lenore covertly watched Steven proceed to the airy living room. He glanced around deliberately, his perceptive gaze seeming to absorb every nuance of the surroundings. After silently studying the photographic decor, he lifted one for closer scrutiny.

Lenore's breath caught. She couldn't see which picture he was holding, yet she knew. It was a strange sensation, almost as though the two men who shared her dreams now occupied the same physical space. In a sense, they did.

"Your husband?" Steven asked without looking up.

"Yes." Her voice sounded strange, husky and somewhat broken.

"He was very young."

"Yes," she whispered. "We both were."

If Steven noticed her tension, he chose not to comment and for that she was grateful. She was torn, divided by two invisible yet equally powerful forces. It was an unpleasant sensation and Lenore was relieved when Steven carefully replaced the photograph and moved toward the French doors.

He stared beyond the wooded yard to the surrounding forest. "I didn't realize how remote this area was."

"Lovely, isn't it?" Lenore replied wistfully. "There's a seasonal stream down in the ravine and there must be fifty species of native trees. Every time I hike into the forest, I find something new and wonderful—a totally different type of fern growing in the bark of a rotted oak, or a wildflower that I'd never seen before. It's like visiting another world. Sometimes I spend an entire day just following the deer paths and—why are you making that crinkly face?"

Arms crossed like bulging shields, Steven's expression mirrored his distaste. "Crawling over putrid wood to stare at weeds isn't my idea of a swell time, that's all."

"That's odd. Most men adore hiking through the wilderness, communing with nature, beating their chests and generally feeling like a macho reincarnation of Daniel Boone."

Steven stared at Lenore as though she'd gone stark, raving mad. "As far as I'm concerned, hiking is a sport reserved for those who can't catch a cab and as for the wilderness . . ." He peered through the glass doors, suspiciously eyeing the brushy ravine. "It's all a bit primitive for my taste."

The incongruous comment struck Lenore as funny. She laughed, picturing the ancient, one-room boat tethered to a decaying dock. "At least I won't wake up after a storm and find myself in Bora Bora. Why anyone would live on that rickety, barnacled hunk of floating flotsam is beyond me."

"I see your point." To her surprise, Steven actually smiled. "The *Bohemian* used to be my uncle's. I had some great times on her when I was a kid. Maybe I'm trying to relive my childhood. Then again, maybe I just like knowing that if I ever get bored with the view I can always pull anchor and change scenery."

Lenore nodded knowingly. "It's the rebel in you. Even though you take on the responsibility and pressures of running a business, there's a contrary side of you that just naturally balks at being another one of society's clones."

The astute observation had a surprising effect on Steven. His expression remained impassive, but his eyes reflected first shock, then wariness. He spoke with strained formality. "If you're through analyzing my Cancerian personality, I'd like to thank you for agreeing to see me."

She managed a casual shrug. "You said it was important. I still don't see why we couldn't talk over the phone."

Hooking his thumbs in his ragged pockets, Steven took a deep breath and exhaled slowly. "I wanted to apologize in person."

Taken aback, Lenore could only stammer, "Apologize for what?"

He hesitated, then glanced away and absently scratched his chin. "I haven't been fair to you or to your grandmother," he explained quietly. "Caution is part of my nature, but I may have misjudged you both. If so, I'm sorry."

The unexpected admission caught Lenore off guard. "Misjudged?"

He shifted awkwardly. "I had some reservations."

"What kind of reservations?" she inquired sweetly. He shrugged and looked so pathetically uncomfortable that Lenore decided to let him off the hook. "You assumed the worst, didn't you? Well, never mind. I understand a suspicious nature because—" Quickly she clamped her mouth shut.

Steven accurately interpreted and finished her thought. "Because you don't trust my uncle—or me—any farther than you can skip-toss a backhoe and I don't blame you. Considering how I imposed myself on you the other day, I can appreciate your feelings."

Remembering their intimate kiss, Lenore felt an annoying flush creep up her throat. She didn't want him to realize how deeply that moment had affected her and idly waved the subject away. "It was a momentary indiscretion, nothing more."

"Of course," he agreed quickly. "Just one of those things."

Lenore managed a bright smile. "Absolutely."

"And there's no reason at all why we can't continue to work together on our, er, mutual problem."

Her smile flattened. No matter what kind of scheme he was hatching, the sly gleam in those lunar eyes meant trouble. She wasn't at all certain that she was up to the challenge but since her options were limited, she met his gaze directly and lifted her chin. "What exactly did you have in mind?"

He answered with a devious grin.

As the *Bohemian* heaved and hawed over the choppy Pacific swells, Lenore hooked one limp arm over the starboard rail and leaned against the tolerant dog standing beside her. She miserably sat on the deck, laid her clammy cheek against Butch's shoulder and moaned softly.

Hell would be like this, she decided. Popular theory envisioned steam exploding from molten rock and searing flame, but Lenore suspected that any unfortunate soul so condemned would spend eternity in stomach-churning agony, pitching and rolling on the waves of purgatory. The mere thought was terrifying and she silently vowed to eliminate any character flaws hampering eventual arrival at a more hospitable destination.

Assuming, of course, that she survived her current ordeal long enough to effect significant improvement. That was doubtful.

From what seemed a great distance, Lenore was vaguely aware of Hettie's ebullient voice and Edison's jaunty laughter. They were fishing off the stern and obviously having a swell time. Even though they were only a few feet away, Lenore's ears roared like a stormy surf and she was much too woozy to concentrate on conversational content.

Suddenly the deck tilted, rocked backward, then lurched to the port side. Lenore made a throaty sound and tightened her grip on the stoic dog. With a sympathetic whine, Butch swung his massive head around and gently licked her face.

A shadow suddenly blocked the sun's unrelenting glare and Lenore painfully squinted up. Judging from the shoulder size, the backlit outline looming overhead must be Steven. Even in her weakened state, she felt a tingle at the sight of him and silently reproached herself. So what if the man had enough sex appeal to fuel a small city? He was obviously deranged or he wouldn't live on this medieval torture device.

Crazy or not, she had to deal with Steven for her grandmother's sake but their relationship was purely functional and Lenore was determined to keep it that way. It hadn't been easy. His penetrating green gaze had the power to obliterate her most implacable resolve but now Lenore's misery proved an effective shield. At the moment, she wanted only to survive this sickening ordeal.

Finally Steven spoke, his voice dripping with empathy and the merest touch of amusement. "How are you feeling?"

"Like a pounded flounder." She suppressed an unlady-like burp and propped her head against Butch's flank. "Go away."

Ignoring her pitiful command, he squatted down and brushed his knuckles across her cheek. "Poor baby," he murmured. "You really are sick, aren't you?"

She gave him a slitty-eyed stare. "Not at all. Butch and I are just sharing quality time."

To Steven's credit, only his eyes smiled. Then he glanced over his shoulder and noted that the two seniors were engrossed in untangling a recalcitrant fishing line. Leaning forward, he lowered his voice. "I could have handled this alone, you know."

Lenore managed to shake her head without throwing up. "No," she mumbled feebly. "The whole idea of planning activities to keep Grandma and Edison busy was so we could *both* keep an eye on them."

"And it's been working, hasn't it?"

Lenore offered a listless shrug. Although it galled her to admit it, Steven's scheme actually *had* been rather effective. Since Hettie and Sonny had returned from their cruise, Steven and Lenore had stuck to their respective relatives like glue, rationalizing that a smoldering romance wouldn't flare in a crowd. Not that Lenore conceded that said romance existed anywhere beyond Steven's overactive imagination, but caution was a virtue when a loved one's welfare is at stake.

So every evening after work, Lenore had rushed straight to Hettie's and Steven had gone directly to Edison's. Ignoring the older couple's polite hints, Lenore and Steven had adhered themselves with the tenacity and nuisance value of stepped-on gum.

Everything had gone according to plan...until Edison had asked to borrow the boat and introduce Hettie to the dubious joys of ocean fishing. Steven had instantly sprung into action, lying through his perfect white teeth and professing that Lenore had frequently expressed a similar desire.

Before she could grab Steven's traitorous throat, the plans had been laid and the deed had been done.

Now she opened one eye and looked up at him. "I'll get you for this."

He spread his hands helplessly. "I didn't know this would happen. Why didn't you tell me?"

"As though I had a chance." She rubbed her eyelids with the back of her hand. "Besides, didn't you see Grandma's expression when you said I wanted—"

"Shh!" Steven warned, then pasted on a welcoming smile and gazed over Lenore's shoulder. She dizzily turned and saw that Hettie and Edison were crossing the deck.

"My stars," Hettie gushed. "Why, this is so much fun it should be illegal. The blue sky and the fresh air, gracious, it's enough to put the bounce back into these stiff old bones."

Edison's eyes twinkled as he bent to whisper in Hettie's pink little ear. Instantly, the older woman flushed prettily and lightly slapped Edison's lean shoulder. "Behave yourself, Sonny. What kind of example is that to set for these fine young people?"

The older man grinned unrepentantly.

Hettie clucked in mock disapproval, then turned her attention to Lenore. "Goodness, the afternoon is almost over and you haven't even dropped a line in the water. Why don't you show these boys what a real fisherman can do, dear? Steven, I'll bet you'd be surprised to know that Lenore won Lake Isabella's big-mouth bass competition two years in a row."

"Big mouth, hmm?" Steven hitched one brow and ignored Lenore's warning stare. "No, that doesn't surprise me at all."

"Oh, my yes," Hettie bubbled. "Of course, she was just a child at the time and ocean fishing *is* a bit different, isn't it, dear?" Pausing, Hettie regarded Lenore with exaggerated solicitude. "By the way, is your tummy any calmer?"

One look at her grandmother's smug expression convinced Lenore that the sharp-witted woman hadn't forgotten the Catalina incident. Worse, Lenore suspected that

Hettie had probably recognized the elaborate deception from its inception and had gone along only because it had amused her to do so.

Lenore managed a wan smile. "I'm feeling much better," she lied. The fact that Steven was having great difficulty maintaining a straight face irritated Lenore immensely. If it weren't for the fact that she was too weak to stand and too sick to care, the man would definitely be shark bait.

But there were other, even more satisfying ways to get even and Lenore's mind hummed with devious abandon. Finally she concocted the perfect plan, ingenious yet exquisitely simple. All she had to do was make sure that the next outing was on her turf. Nature would do the rest.

Lenore could hardly wait.

Picking her way cautiously along the steep path, Lenore steadied herself on an oak limb and stepped around a jutting rock. She heard a muffled grunt behind her and bit back a smile as she glanced over her shoulder. Although she saw nothing but thick brush, she knew Steven was close by, struggling his way through the alien landscape. "Be careful of low branches," she called cheerfully.

Steven's garbled response was succinct and, Lenore suspected, not particularly civil. She grinned happily and listened to the sounds of cracking twigs and footsteps through the dense carpet of dried leaves. Patiently she waited, not wanting to miss a single, satisfying moment of Steven's discomfort.

Butch appeared first, panting and pooped, squeezing his blocky body between two thick, thorned bushes. The poor animal was obviously out of his element and Lenore felt a twinge of guilt over the dog's distress. After all, it wasn't Butch's fault that his master needed a lesson in humility.

Paddling up the trail, Butch paused occasionally to sniff odd animal scents clinging to the foliage. When he reached Lenore, he leaned against her thigh and stared up pitifully.

"Poor old guy," Lenore mumbled, scratching one floppy ear. "You'd rather be stretched out on a smooth deck catching a few rays, wouldn't you?"

Tongue lolling, the tired animal rolled his eyes and snorted in apparent agreement.

"I know it's been a tough day, but if you can make it another half mile to the house, you'll get a nice cool bowl of water."

Appearing tantalized by the prospect, Butch immediately stood, licked his wiskers and lumbered up the trail. Lenore was contemplating whether to follow the dog or continue waiting for Steven when she heard another loud snap, followed by an angry barrage of colorful epithets.

She couldn't see Steven but knew from the sound that he was right behind the thorned bushes. After a moment, he called out to her. "It looks like something has been rooting around back here."

"You mean those groves and mounds in the dirt?"

"Yeah. Gophers?"

"No, pigs."

There was a moment's silence before he spoke again. "Who keeps livestock down here?"

"Nobody. They're wild pigs."

The silence was longer this time and when he finally spoke, his voice had an odd tremor. "You mean . . . boars? The kind with tusks?"

"Uh-huh. There are dozens of them down here, maybe even hundreds. Some of them weigh four hundred pounds but don't worry. They're only dangerous if they see you first. Of course, you're making so much noise they're probably circling now for a coordinated attack—"

Steven came thrashing through the brush, cursing and flailing as thorny limbs captured his T-shirt. He swore and gave his arm a mighty yank. The sleeve ripped from shoulder to hem and Steven stomped toward Lenore, scowling darkly.

Instantly Lenore pointed toward the pathway directly in front of his feet. "Watch out for the—"

With a surprised bellow, Steven tripped, grabbing a hanging limb, which broke off in his hand, then he lurched forward and sprawled across the path like a prostrate monk at prayer.

"—Rock," Lenore finished lamely.

Lifting his face from the layer of crisp leaves, he glared up and spoke through tightly clenched teeth. "Thank you."

"You're, ah, welcome." She turned away for a moment, trying desperately not to laugh. By the time she'd composed herself, Steven had levered into a sitting position and was plucking twigs out of his clothing. She knelt down. "Are you okay?"

"Oh, sure," he snapped, snatching up the leafy bough broken in the futile attempt to catch himself. "I love rubbing my face in dirt and I'll never miss all that skin I *used* to have on my knees." To emphasize his displeasure, he shook the limb in Lenore's direction. "But what the hell, my clothes are almost dry after that refreshing, although unexpected, dip in the creek and the swelling is almost gone from my ankle. I probably won't need a body cast after all."

"I'm glad you're enjoying yourself." Carefully avoiding the green foliage, Lenore moved his hand and the offending branch away from her face. "How would you feel about a nice, juicy skin rash?"

His expression flickered from annoyance to apprehension as he followed her gaze to the bushy limb he held. "Oh, no."

Lenore confirmed his fears with as much sympathy as she could muster. "I'm afraid so. That's poison oak."

He stared at the branch as though it were a snake then flung it into the ravine and leaped to his feet, scrutinizing his palms with obvious agitation. "Do you think I'll get a rash?"

She shrugged. "Does a fish get wet?"

Ignoring his black stare, she grinned cheerfully then stood and made a production of brushing off her jeans. "It won't show up for a day or two. After that, it'll only drive you crazy for one, maybe two weeks." His jaw sagged and she patted his cheek. "Just don't scratch or you'll have blisters in places you don't even want to think about. It spreads, you know."

Steven couldn't look more horrified if she'd told him that his ears would fall off at midnight. "Blisters?"

"Umm. Kind of like chicken pox, only smaller." She pulled a dried oak leaf from his hair. "Gosh, this is almost as much fun as throwing up over a deck rail, isn't it? Well, we'd better get moving. Grandma and Edison are probably back at the house by now."

Not waiting for a response, Lenore spun around and headed briskly down the winding path. She could almost feel Steven's furious gaze on the back of her neck but oddly enough, it was all she could do to keep from whistling.

So engrossed was Lenore in her own thoughts that she didn't hear Steven gaining on her and was startled when he suddenly grasped her shoulders from behind. She lurched to a stop and he spun her around.

His face was inches from hers. "You're really enjoying this, aren't you?"

"Oh, yes."

"There's one thing you don't know about me, honey," he said in a whispered growl that sent goose bumps down her spine. "I never suffer alone."

For a moment she was mesmerized by the power of eyes so green that the forest paled in comparison. His nearness weakened her knees and the warmth radiating from his powerful body penetrated her emotional shield, igniting a disturbing liquid heat deep inside her. His scent enveloped her, a dusky odor of pine and oak and potent masculine desire.

Even before his mouth moved closer to hers, she knew he was going to kiss her. Part of her screamed that she should turn away and run as though her very life depended on it.

Because her life did depend on it. His lips would brand her, sear a place in her heart that would belong only to him and that frightened her half to death.

Or at least it should.

But at that moment, all those crazy disjointed thoughts were relegated to a distant corner of her mind. She was conscious only of his mouth moving purposely closer and closer still, and she was crazed with anticipation.

When his lips brushed hers, the shock wave hit like a bolt of white lightning. She couldn't breathe, she couldn't move, she was helpless to fight the explosion of mounting passion.

Steven's kiss deepened and Lenore responded without thought. Suddenly she was terrified that he might withdraw and she clutched him with renewed urgency.

The world spun like a crazy top and her mind whirled with it. She was frantic with desire, driven by blind emotion and long-suppressed need, helplessly locked in the intractable grip of something so powerful yet so glorious that she was transported beyond the realm of her own accepted reality. The universe twisted, collapsing on itself while stars burst with psychedelic brilliance. She was overwhelmed by the magic, the rapturous joy. Even with Michael, she'd never experienced such—

Lenore stiffened. Dear Lord, what was she doing?

Had she forgotten that the joy of having loved Michael had never overcome the agonizing grief of his loss? With love, loss was inevitable.

Shakily she pulled away, swallowing a disappointed whimper when the kiss was broken. Steven took a ragged breath and she went rigid. Steven lifted his head but seemed loath to loosen his grip. His eyes asked the silent questions as he absently stroked her bare arms. Moistening her lips, Lenore looked down at the strong hands caressing her skin with such tenderness.

Steven followed her gaze, then released her so suddenly that she rocked backward. Obviously dismayed, he jammed his contaminated hands into his pockets. "Have...I infected you?"

Because she was still reeling from the impact of his kiss, she thought he'd said "affected" rather than "infected" and was blown away by his gall. He *had* affected her, of course, but she'd have rather dueled a boar with a toothpick than to let him know that. Still her voice conveyed a disheartening lack of conviction. "Not at all. I'm immune."

"To poison oak—or to me?"

Momentarily baffled by the odd response, Lenore suddenly realized that the strong palms that had been brushing her skin with such sensuality had been coated with toxic sap. She managed to meet his gaze without wavering. "Both."

As Lenore stepped away Steven noted her unsteady gait and glazed expression. Their eyes met and her pensive gaze offered a fleeting glimpse of her secret vulnerability and of her pain. Then she whirled quickly and disappeared up the trail.

Shaken, Steven leaned against a red cedar and took a cleansing breath. He hadn't planned to kiss her. It just happened. Now he was standing here feeling as though he'd been mule-kicked and he didn't have a clue as to why. What was wrong with him, anyway? Even if he was looking for romantic entanglements—which he most definitely was not—Lenore Gregory Blaine was the worst possible choice. Except for a shared desire to protect their loved ones, they had about as much in common as a mouse and a moose.

Good Lord, the woman actually got her jollies by trekking through pig-infested wilderness. She was most certainly nuts, so why in the world did he feel as though an intrinsic part of him had just been surgically altered?

With a perplexed sigh, Steven tugged at his earlobe and sorted through the odd rush of conflicting emotions.

Lenore wasn't like any other woman he'd ever met. She wasn't flirtatious or coquettish and didn't fall into a coma when her hair got wet or her makeup smeared. She was spunky and Steven respected that, but what he felt now went beyond mere admiration. At least, he thought it did.

The word love popped into his mind and he instantly dismissed it. Steven had a rotten track record with love and the mere thought of it made him sweat like a cornered coward. With the exception of Edison, every person Steven ever cared about had betrayed and abandoned him—his parents, Lucinda, even Crazy Old Sam.

So to Steven love was simply an obscure word for which the dictionary lacked appropriate definition. People "love" animals and popcorn and the latest bestseller. The fact that Steven felt something for Lenore was indisputable but he was completely unwilling to consider that his feelings went deeper than mere sexual attraction.

Sex was simply biology and he could deal with that.

But something else was happening here, something powerful and frightening. Steven didn't know what in hell was going on. He didn't like what was happening to him but he didn't know how to stop it, either.

And that scared the hell out of him.

Chapter Seven

Steven unrolled the blueprints on a plywood platform and used small hunks of broken concrete to flatten the curled corners. He tried to concentrate but the lines blurred and his mind wandered. Across the site, jackhammers pounded solid rock until the soles of his feet vibrated with every pulsing blow. The rifle-crack of air tools was nearly drowned out by the diesel whine of heavy equipment and the entire construction site sounded like a war zone.

Oblivious to the deafening cacophony, Steven absently scratched his itchy palm, stared sightlessly at the blue-lined specifications and thought about Lenore. He could still smell her fresh fragrance and taste the sweet softness of her mouth. She'd felt so fragile in his arms, yet she'd responded to his kiss with a fervency that made his pulse race and his blood boil.

For two days, he'd tried to get her out of his mind and for two nights, he'd lain awake with her image burning in his brain. If he'd been the superstitious type, he'd have sworn that he was bewitched. Maybe she was a sorceress. Maybe poison oak was an aphrodisiac.

Maybe he'd completely lost his mind.

"Hey, boss man!"

Annoyed, Steven glared at the beefy crew chief lumbering toward him. "What now?" he snapped, not bothering to conceal his exasperation at the interruption.

Chester wasn't the least bit intimidated and continued his unhurried pace. When he finally reached Steven, he massaged his thick belly and gazed idly around the job site. "Crane's fixed."

Since Steven was still distracted by thoughts of Lenore, the significance of the cryptic comment eluded him. "Crane?"

The crew chief raised a hairy eyebrow. "Yeah. That tall sucker with the big yellow arm."

Steven moaned. The huge crane in question was used to hoist iron beams into position and had been felled by hydraulic problems last week, throwing the development even further behind schedule. Repairing that piece of equipment had been his number one priority... or at least, it should have been.

He shook his head, hoping to exorcise thoughts of Lenore so he could drag his mind back to the business at hand. The gesture was futile and Steven was royally ticked by his own weakness.

"Watcha want us to do with her?"

Steven frowned. "With whom?"

Rocking back on his heels, Chester gave Steven a disgusted look then jerked his thumb in the direction of the massive machine.

"Oh." Lifting his hard hat, Steven wiped his brow and silently cursed the invading dimpled image. He felt powerless and that angered him. "Well, I sure as hell don't want you to pick apples with the damned thing," Steven finally growled. "We're supposed to have a four-level parking structure ready for inspection by the end of the month. Authorize whatever overtime it takes to have the first floor ready for joists by tomorrow morning."

"Can't do that."

This was too much for a crabby contractor with shattered nerves. Teeth clenched, jaw twitching, Steven fixed the insubordinate crew chief with the hard stare that routinely cowed lesser men. "You'll get that lousy crane into position and start pulling iron or I'll damn well find someone who can."

With a shrug, the chief scratched himself then met Steven's furious gaze with one of cool defiance. "Do what you got to do," he said quietly. "But I ain't sending no crane to dangle a two-ton beam over them poor fools down in the hole."

Steven felt like every drop of blood had suddenly drained from his body. "Oh, God," he whispered. "The foundation crew."

Chester spit in the dirt. "Yep."

Weakly, Steven turned away and tried to compose himself. When the crane had malfunctioned, the schedule had been shuffled to minimize time loss. Dear Lord, how could he have forgotten? It had been Steven's decision to pour the basement slab during the crane's downtime and yet he'd just given an order that would have seriously endangered the half-dozen men who were carrying out those original instructions.

Steven wiped his dripping forehead. "Move the crane into the south lot until the concrete work is completed."

With an ambivalent nod, Chester ambled away and for the first time since he'd hired the slovenly crew chief, Steven was actually grateful for the man's obstinance. A more accommodating supervisor might have actually carried out Steven's dangerous order and the thought made him shudder.

Suddenly Steven was inexplicably angry. His life had spiraled out of control. He was angry with Lenore for having encroached upon the sanctity of his private thoughts and he was angry with himself for allowing her to do so.

He couldn't understand this unquenchable obsession. Yes, Lenore was pretty but Steven had known more beautiful women. Besides, chatty people had always irritated him; when Lenore jabbered like a magpie, he was overwhelmed by an irrational desire to kiss her silly.

So maybe he just had a bad case of the hots. A crude analogy, but one Steven could deal with. After all, passion was not an unconquerable weakness. One thing Edison had always counseled was maintaining strict control of one's rampaging hormones.

"Biological urges are a fact of nature," he'd warned. "Either you control them or they'll control you and many a fine young man has found himself kneeling at an altar because he hadn't learned the difference between basic science and romantic fairy tales."

As always, Edison had repeatedly been proven right. Over the years, Steven had watched from a discreet distance as intelligent men and women married, then turned sullen and self-absorbed. There was no blame to be laid. Marriage and misery just naturally went hand in hand.

But the tender trap *could* be avoided. His uncle was living proof. Edison was the last bachelor, a man content in his own skin and by scrupulously emulating his role model, Steven was determined to get Lenore Gregory Blaine out of his system once and for all.

"Steven!" Lenore took a surprised step backward, her hand still grasping the front doorknob. "You're supposed to be with Edison tonight."

Without waiting for an invitation, Steven strode into the foyer. "Edison can take care of himself," he announced firmly, pleased that his voice reinforced his resolve.

After a stunned moment, Lenore pushed the door shut with more force than necessary. "It's not your uncle I'm worried about. Besides, we had a deal."

Shielding himself with folded arms, Steven managed to face her without melting inside. That was definitely a good sign, he decided and was buoyed by the perceived victory. He squared his shoulders and regarded her with feigned detachment. "The deal is off."

Her eyes widened, then narrowed suspiciously. "Just like that?"

"Just like that." He caught a fleeting glimpse of confusion in her eyes before she looked away and absently ouched her abdomen. The protective gesture affected him nd he felt compelled to explain. "I realize that it was never Hettie's intent to hoodwink my uncle out of his life savngs—"

"Of course not!"

"So you can see that there's no need to continue this landestine charade."

"Oh, really?" Hands on hips, Lenore lifted her chin and ave him a killing stare. "What about your uncle's intenions toward my grandmother?"

Steven shrugged. "He likes her."

"Of course he likes her! Everyone likes her but that's not he point, is it?" With a sound of disgust, Lenore paced the mall living room and muttered incoherently.

Her agitation upset Steven and he was irritated that the voman had managed to penetrate his newly fortified deenses. "Exactly what *is* the point here?" he demanded harply. "Do you think that any man who looks twice is loomed to fall in love? Well, don't kid yourself, honey. Not very guy trips over his heart because a pretty woman ofers a dimpled smile, and an innocent kiss is *not* a one-way icket to the altar. People aren't helpless victims. We have hoices. We can control our emotions. That's what sepaates us from animals."

Lenore stared blankly. "What on earth are you talking bout?"

He cleared his throat and shifted nervously. "I just meant hat my uncle is an expert at avoiding emotional entangleents. Say, it's awfully warm in here, isn't it? Maybe you hould open a window or something."

The fact that Lenore was looking at him as though he'd prouted antlers added to Steven's discomfort. Finally she valked across the room and opened the French doors. A ool breeze brushed his face and he sighed. This wasn't going well. Once again he'd lost control of the situation and hat bothered him immensely.

It should have all been so simple. After hours of intense oncentration, Steven had hatched the perfect scheme to lisplay his indifference. He would calmly inform Lenore that since this chaperone business had been a mistake, there was no reason for them to see each other again.

But that's where his mental script had ended. He hadn considered her response. Would she be angry? Disappointed? Or even worse, would she be relieved?

At the moment, she was gazing through the open door with a faraway expression that created a peculiar tingling sensation in his chest. Steven fidgeted and wished to hell h could just offer a breezy "adios" and leave skid marks. But he was trapped, not by any tangible prison but by an ur fathomable need to be with her.

Before he could analyze the implications of that surprising development, Lenore stepped away from the door an leaned against the wall. She looked up with an expression of hurt and bewilderment that made him feel like the scum of the earth.

He stretched out his hand in a gesture that begged under standing. "Please don't worry about Hettie. My uncle is gentleman."

She cocked her head and raised one neat eyebrow. "Is your contention that taking *polite* advantage of a vulnerable old woman is acceptable?"

"Oh, for crying out loud—"

"Because if so, I've got a news flash for you, bucko. I'n not about to stand back and let that happen. Grandma ha been through enough." Lenore pushed away from the wa and strode furiously toward Steven. "If you want to bac out of our agreement, that's fine. I don't need your help bu understand this—I intend to protect my grandmother, wit or without you." She punctuated her statement by pressin one pink finger against Steven's chest.

Frustrated, Steven grabbed her hand and held it a sa distance away. "What do you think Edison is going to d throw Hettie over his shoulder and haul her off to his cave Good Lord, woman, this is the twentieth century. Nothin is going to happen that she doesn't want to happen." strange expression crossed Lenore's face and she stumble back a step. Reluctantly Steven released her hand. Sh swallowed hard and he noticed the slight tremor of he slender shoulders. "That's it, isn't it? You're afraid your grandmother is falling for Edison."

She feebly shook her head and whispered, "No."

"Yes it is. I can see it in your face. You know that Hettie *wants* Edison and that scares the hell out of you, doesn't it?"

"That's disgusting," Lenore snapped. "My grandmother is not a tart and how dare you imply that she is?"

Angrily she spun around and Steven instantly took hold of her arm. She stopped abruptly but refused to look at him.

"I'm not implying anything of the kind," Steven intoned with exaggerated patience. "Two people being attracted to each other is the most natural thing in the world."

Lenore yanked away from Steven's grasp and folded her arms tightly. "Grandma is *not* attracted to Edison—or anyone else, for that matter."

"How can you be so sure?"

"Because I know how much she loved my grandfather and how she grieved when he died. She would never deliberately expose herself to that kind of pain again. No one would." Her final words were muffled. Turning quickly, her elbow brushed the neat row of photographs on the sofa table and a single frame fell over. Lenore froze, staring at the flattened picture. She was as white as a snowbank.

Steven instinctively knew that the downed photograph was of Lenore's husband and fought an inexplicable surge of resentment. Not that Steven was jealous, of course. The poor fellow was dead, after all, and hostility toward a ghost was not only insensitive, but it was downright stupid. Besides, if Lenore had loved the guy, he must of been one hell of a man.

The thought made Steven's stomach knot painfully.

Replacing the photograph to its original position, Steven posed a deceptively casual question. "How long were you married?"

Still staring at the picture, Lenore moistened her lips. "Eight months."

"That's all? I mean, you still seem so broken up, I just assumed that, well..." His voice trailed off and he shrugged helplessly.

To his surprise, Lenore didn't seem offended by his bumbling response. "We didn't have much time together," she acknowledged quietly. "I've always thought that unfair."

That was probably an understatement. Dying young was always a tragedy but this man had missed a lifetime with Lenore and that made his loss even more grievous. "What happened to him?"

"There was an accident."

"Automobile?"

She shook her head. "He worked at the refinery over on Pacific Coast Highway. A pressure valve failed and one of the pipes sprang a leak. I don't understand all the technical aspects. All I know is that there was a spark, flames and an explosion. Six men died. Michael was one of them."

As she spoke, Steven observed every nuance of her body language. On the surface she seemed impassive, almost detached, but there was an innate sadness in her eyes that seemed vaguely familiar.

Then he remembered.

They had been in the hospital parking lot, the night of the disastrous ball game. He recalled the sound of wailing sirens and how she had watched the glowing horizon with such obvious horror. Suddenly he had a revolting thought. "You saw it happen, didn't you?"

He held his breath, hoping he was wrong.

"Yes," she whispered. "We only lived a couple blocks away."

Steven moaned, sickened by the realization of what she must have endured.

Lenore sat stiffly on the sofa, her eyes focused somewhere in time. "At first I thought it was an earthquake. Things flew out of cupboards and every mirror in the house cracked. But when I went to the balcony, I could see the flames." She spoke methodically, without emotion, as though reciting a script of someone else's life. "The smoke was so black and there was this horrible smell and I heard sirens coming closer and closer—"

She paused as Steven sat beside her. He held her hand, warming her icy skin between his palms. She didn't object. But then, she didn't even seem aware of his presence.

"The next thing I remember, I was pushing through the crowd of people outside the refinery gate. A policeman told me to leave, but I ducked under his arm and ran toward the building where Michael worked. There wasn't much left of it. Two firefighters came out of the debris carrying a body. There wasn't much left of that, either." Her voice caught and tears glistened against her pale skin. "I . . . don't think it was Michael."

The image of Lenore standing alone, helpless and hysterical, watching emergency crews search for pieces of her husband was almost more than Steven could stomach. He didn't trust his voice and wouldn't have known what to say anyway, so he simply brushed away a wet strand of her hair and gently kissed her cheek.

She shuddered and closed her eyes, squeezing out a fresh trickle of tears. "It was my fault," she whispered. "He died because of me."

The startling statement nearly choked him. He stiffened. "My God, the explosion was a horrible accident but you couldn't stop it. How can you possibly believe—"

"You don't understand," she moaned, pulling her hand away and covering her face with her palms. "We had this stupid fight. We screamed at each other and said terrible things."

"People argue. It's never pretty but it happens all the time."

"Not to us. Michael and I rarely argued. He was always so mellow, nothing really bothered him. His only fault was that he loved his job too much and I was jealous." Sniffing, she lowered her hands and gazed up with reddened eyes. "That's what we were arguing about that afternoon. I was being totally unreasonable and generally behaving like a spoiled brat. Then I took off my wedding ring and threw it, saying that if his job was more important than me, he should try sleeping with it. He put the ring into his pocket and left." She looked away. "I never saw him again."

Because he couldn't think of anything else to do, Steven put his arms around her and felt her shudder once before melting against his chest. Her damp cheek rested against his shoulder and when she continued to tremble, he was overwhelmed by the urge to offer comfort. But because he could do nothing to exorcise her terrible grief, he shared it.

He understood why she concealed emotion with humor and had such a phobic fear of relationships. Everything made sense now.

"Shh," he whispered, caressing her soft hair. "I know how badly it hurts. You can't forget the cruel words but you can't take them back, either. That day is history. If you can't live with that, the guilt will tear you up inside."

She shivered violently then used his shoulder to lever upright and looked straight at him. For a moment, she said nothing, simply searched his eyes with laser intensity. Then she finally spoke so softly that he could barely hear. "Grandma told me about your parents," she whispered. "I'm so sorry."

"It . . . was a long time ago."

"Does that help?"

"No." He sighed. "Are you suggesting that I doctor my own ills before I try ministering to yours?"

"That isn't what I meant. It's just that, for years people have been telling me that I should forget what happened. Because of all you had suffered, you realized that I couldn't do that. You understand guilt because, like me, you live with it every day of your life."

Steven closed his eyes and tried to shake off the memories she had evoked. Lenore was right. He *did* understand the guilt. God knows, not a day had gone by in the past twenty-eight years that he hadn't regretted what had happened so long ago. He could still picture himself as a child, eavesdropping while his screaming parents castigated each other, using their son as the weapon of cruel accusations and dire threats.

Then, with angry tears staining his dirty little face, he'd crept out his bedroom window and disappeared into the night. And because of that cowardly act, his parents had lied. From that moment on, guilt had been his shadow and shame had been his constant companion.

Yes, he understood Lenore's pain and for the first time in his life, he knew that someone understood his. He and Lenore shared an emotional connection now, a spiritual bonding that was more intimate than the sexual act itself.

For minutes, maybe even hours, they communicated with silent eyes. Only when Lenore looked down and lifted his hand did Steven realize that he'd been absently rubbing his palm against the rough denim covering his thigh.

Gently she turned his hand, cooing sympathetically when she saw the blistered rash. Her touch was delicate and delicious. He tried not to breathe, afraid the slightest movement would cause her to withdraw.

She was so close he could smell the tantalizing fragrance of her hair and see the fine texture of her tanned skin. She wore a silky, sleeveless top that clung to her shapely breasts while the dipping neckline offered a teasing peek of the creamy rounded flesh beneath.

Suddenly she released his hand and shivered as though chilled, then warmed herself by rubbing her arms. Steven's gaze followed the movement and he saw the rash, a scalded patch on her upper arm that was a mirror image of his own swollen palm.

Gently tracing around the mottled area with his fingertip, Steven whispered, "I guess neither one of us is immune."

Raising her head slightly, she moistened her lips. "I . . . guess not."

Cupping her chin between his thumb and forefinger, he lifted her face, hesitating only briefly before claiming her soft mouth. She tasted even sweeter than he remembered and when she parted her lips, his exploration deepened. A tiny whimper bubbled from deep inside her and she wound her arms around his neck with a frenzy that drove him wild.

He wanted her. Dear God, he'd never wanted anything in his life as much as he wanted this woman. Right now, right here, completely and forever.

With a quick twist, Steven lowered Lenore to the sofa. Embracing him, she dragged him down and covered his face with her mouth, kissing him frantically. Steven was swept away with the power of their passion, aware only of the feel of her firm body writhing beneath him and the desperate pounding of his own heart.

He cupped one soft breast and shuddered with exquisite pleasure as her hardened nipple pressed against his palm. She moaned and arched upward, allowing him to pull up her blouse. After a moment's fumbling, the wispy bra fell away and he gasped, overcome by her beauty. He caressed her bare breasts, using his thumb to circle the dusky nipple until her head thrashed and she dug her fingers into his back. When he lowered his mouth, she cried out in ecstasy.

Lenore was crazed with desire, unable to focus on anything but the exquisite sensations. She was dissolving, becoming one with the man whose touch had such incredible power over her mind and body. His gentle fingers cleansed her blemished soul and she felt free, her spirit soaring with unbridled joy.

Part of herself called out a sullen warning that she was in danger of losing something she valued—her emotional independence. She ignored her own silent plea. The call of passion was too strong. This was not simply a man. This was Steven and he had awakened the sleeping giant inside her.

Lenore wanted him and for this moment, this glorious moment, there was no shame in that need.

But the moment was all too brief.

Even before his body stiffened, she felt his withdrawal. When he moved away, she wanted desperately to stop him, to reach out and surrender to his comforting warmth. She wanted to, but she didn't.

Steven stood and turned away, holding his head between his palms as though expecting his skull to explode. Then he groaned, an anguished moan of despair that sent an ominous chill down her spine.

With some effort, she managed to speak. "What…is it?"

At the sound of her voice, he stiffened and swore under his breath. His hands fell to his side but he didn't turn, wouldn't face her. "I didn't want this to happen."

She licked her dry lips and struggled into a sitting position. "I know that. Neither did I."

He raked his hair, shuddered once and without another word, strode across the room and walked out the front door.

The room was deathly quiet then and Lenore felt empty, as though a vital organ had been ruthlessly torn out. She was sick inside, remembering how she'd clung to Steven, how she'd wanted him. And she still did. That was the worst part. That was the betrayal.

She gazed at Michael's photograph and wondered why she couldn't feel guilty. Something was wrong here, something was different. Lenore was different. She had changed inside and nothing made sense anymore. Convictions that had once seemed indisputable were now cloudy and confusing.

But if everything else now seemed elusive and beyond comprehension, of one thing Lenore was absolutely certain.

Nothing in her life would ever be the same again.

Impatiently tapping the linen-draped table, Lenore alternately glanced at her watch and eyed the restaurant's marbled foyer.

The waiter hovered like an annoying insect. "May I bring you something while you're waiting, *mademoiselle*? Hors d'oeuvres or perhaps a cocktail? The rumaki is superb or if you'd prefer something lighter, might I suggest—"

"Nothing, thank you." She softened the interruption with a strained smile. "I'm fine, really."

"As you wish." With a smart bow, the waiter withdrew to one corner of the elegant dining room, clasped his hands and stared sullenly.

Lenore looked at her watch again and wondered if she'd misunderstood the cryptic message on the answering machine. She had nearly convinced herself that Hettie had wanted to meet at *Shea's Eatery* instead of *Chez Cary* when a familiar, tinkling laugh filtered across the room.

Lenore exhaled in relief, then smiled brightly as Hettie, splendidly gowned in flowing chiffon, followed the tuxedoed host across the room. But Lenore's contentment was all too brief and her smile froze when Edison appeared, dressed to the nines and grinning madly.

Lenore's heart sank like a rock. She'd hoped to spend the evening alone with her grandmother. Dining in a fancy restaurant wasn't an everyday occurrence but Lenore and Hettie had indulged themselves occasionally, usually for birthdays and other special events. It wasn't unheard of, however, for the two women to simply celebrate surviving a particularly tough week, so Lenore hadn't given much thought to analyzing the reason for Hettie's invitation.

Now she was disappointed, surprisingly so, but nonetheless managed to suppress her chagrin and greet Edison politely.

After the maître d' seated them, Hettie favored the man with a dazzling smile, then turned to Lenore and launched into a breathless monologue. "You look lovely, dear. My, that's such a stunning outfit. Satin is so elegant and white does bring out the sheen of your hair." Hettie paused long enough to frown disapprovingly. "But the cut is much too conservative for such a beautiful young woman. Why, you're covered up to your chin, for goodness' sake. You needn't conceal the blessings God gave you, child. Show off that gorgeous figure. After all, a modest display of cleavage adds to a woman's mystery, doesn't it, Sonny?"

Edison gazed at Hettie as though the moon sat on her shoulder. "Yes, dear."

"You see?" Hettie crowed. "Now, Lenore, you must promise that you'll go shopping tomorrow and buy something outrageously sexy for yourself."

"Really, Grandma, I don't think—"

"Nonsense, dear. It's my treat and I'll not hear another word about it." Waving away any protest, Hettie pursed her lips and scrutinized Lenore with distressing enthusiasm.

'Something in strapless lace, I think, or perhaps a delicious clingy knit with a plunging neckline. Yes, indeed, that
would do nicely but only if it's not one of those horrid an-
kle-length things that conceal your beautiful assets.'' Hettie sighed dreamily. ''Lordy, what I wouldn't give for such
lovely long legs.''

Edison spoke up. ''The world is full of skinny young
women walking on spindly twigs. Personally I prefer strong,
substantial limbs and a woman of huggable proportions.''

''Gracious me, what a silver-tongued old devil you are.''

Edison responded with a whispered utterance that made
Hettie's cheeks glow like pink light bulbs.

Lenore was too distracted to be alarmed by the affectionate display and self-consciously touched the bodice of her
jewel-necked gown. She wasn't offended by her grandmother's blunt appraisal but she was most certainly surprised by it. Hettie had never commented on Lenore's
apparel before and certainly had never encouraged her—or
anyone else, for that matter—to expose ''cleavage.''

Suddenly Edison called out, ''Steven! Over here, son.''

Lenore felt the blood drain from her face. The minute
she'd seen Edison, she should have realized that Steven
wouldn't be far behind. Part of her longed to spin in her
chair and devour him with her eyes. Another part, the sane
part, admonished her to feign indifference. After all, they
hadn't seen each other since the evening that they'd nearly
initiated her living room sofa in such a shocking manner.
Steven had been the one who'd walked out and without so
much as a fond farewell or a backward glance. That had
been three days ago and they hadn't spoken since.

Now he was here. She could feel his presence move closer
and closer, then his scent surrounded her like loving arms.
A shadow made her shiver and as he stood behind her, his
hesitation as tangible as a touch. Finally the table's only
vacant chair moved and in a heartbeat, he was tautly seated
beside her.

He greeted her with strained formality. ''Good evening,
Lenore.''

"Steven." The brief acknowledgement parched her throat and she reached for her water glass.

"Glad you could make it," Edison said jovially, then raised one hand over his head and loudly snapped his fingers. "*Garçon!* Champagne, *s'il vous plaît,* a bottle of your very finest."

Sneaking a peek over the crystal rim of her glass, Lenore saw Steven wince at his uncle's booming request. Steven looked different somehow, and after a moment she realized that the man was actually wearing a jacket and tie. Granted, the skinny knit tie clashed with his checkered shirt and a corduroy sport coat with leather elbow patches didn't exactly blend with the elegant French ambience; still, it was the first time she'd seen him dressed in anything other than tight jeans and baggy T-shirts.

She had to admit he looked just swell. Of course, Lenore rather liked the tight jeans, too, and decided that he'd probably look sexy wearing a canvas sack. That was depressing. At the moment, he exuded enough animal magnetism to jump-start every feminine heart for six city blocks—including Lenore's—and that irritated her immensely.

If there had been a vaccination against the man's sex appeal, Lenore would have been the first to offer her arm because she was definitely coming down with a bad case of... something.

The waiter appeared with a silver ice bucket and a linen-wrapped bottle. From the corner of her eye, Lenore saw Steven lean stiffly back in his chair. Then he spoke to his uncle, softly but with a definite edge. "I didn't think you cared for champagne."

"It's a special occasion," Edison replied, then tasted the sparkling wine and nodded his approval. The waiter instantly filled four glasses, clicked his polished heels and left.

Frowning, Steven fingered the crystal goblet. "What occasion is that?"

"A toast!" Edison boomed, holding his champagne glass over the center of the table. Hettie lifted her glass and giggled, then both seniors waited patiently until Lenore followed suit. Finally Steven sighed and picked up his glass. Edison smiled. "To the golden years of life and to the beautiful woman who has agreed to spend them with me."

Edison and Hettie clinked their glasses and sipped the bubbling liquid without taking their eyes off each other. Lenore simply sat stiff-armed and in shock, oblivious to the sloshed liquor drizzling down her wrist.

Steven set his glass on the table and fixed Edison with a disbelieving stare. "What...are you saying?"

Gazing dreamily into the older woman's glowing face, Edison kissed her plump little hand. "Hettie has just made me the happiest man in the world by agreeing to be my wife."

"No!" As Lenore's glass crashed to the table, she ignored the mess and stared in absolute horror. "You can't...dear God, how could you even consider—" Her throat closed up without warning and she was paralyzed with shock.

Instantly Edison snatched up a napkin and futilely dabbed at the spreading stain. Bewildered and obviously hurt, Hettie extended a reconciling hand. "Child, what is it? I thought you'd be happy for us."

Lenore automatically recoiled. "How could you do this to Grandpa? You loved him...I know you did. How can you just forget all about him, as though he never even existed?"

Hettie dropped her gaze to the table and when she looked up again, her eyes were sad, yet filled with understanding. "I will always love your grandfather, but I love Sonny, too. The human heart is a wonderful thing, child, with a boundless capacity for love."

Fighting a bizarre inner panic, Lenore twisted her napkin and shook off her grandmother's words. "But you suffered so much when you lost Grandpa. What if Edison dies tomorrow? If you let yourself love him, how could you bear that? Why in God's name would you even take such a chance?"

"Lenore, that's quite unkind," Hettie admonished, patting Edison's knee. The poor man was squirming, obviously distressed by the candid discussion of his own mortality and had Lenore not been so overwrought, she would have been horrified by her insensitivity.

But she was in too much turmoil to be so observant. All she could think about was that if her staid grandmother had fallen victim to the Collier charm, what chance did Lenore have to escape?

Suddenly she couldn't breathe. She had to get out. Now.

Pushing away from the table, she stood so quickly that her chair would have fallen had Steven not steadied it. She tried to speak, to explain, but she was choking inside and in the end, she could do nothing except whirl and dash out of the restaurant.

Steven watched solemnly until Lenore disappeared. He understood her torment and in fact, he shared it. The shocking news had jolted Steven to the soles of his feet. His uncle had been a role model in avoiding affairs of the heart. No matter how Steven had been tempted, he had repeatedly consoled himself that he, like Edison, could control his burgeoning emotions.

To Steven, Edison's announcement was like a defection . . . and a mirror.

Chapter Eight

It was nearly dawn. Lenore poured a cup of tea and watched the first gray light creep over the horizon. Her head throbbed. Her heart ached. She was confused and she was frightened.

What was wrong with her, anyway? Last night at the restaurant, she'd behaved so badly that her stomach turned at the memory. But she hadn't been able to control the sudden fear, the agonizing shock of . . . of what?

Dear God, she didn't know.

Hettie's announcement had been stunning and completely unexpected, but Lenore's inner turmoil had gone well beyond mere astonishment. She'd been devastated. Had her grandmother actually forgotten the grief, the incalculable desolation of Grandpa's death? How could Hettie even consider facing that pain again?

Ten hours of soul-searching had produced only the answer that Lenore feared most. Hettie had lost control of her emotions and in spite of the risks that both women know only too well, her grandmother had fallen in love.

If love could capture a woman of Hettie's intellect and self-determination, then Lenore was surely doomed. For weeks, Steven's image had haunted her. At the most inappropriate moment, Lenore would suddenly recall the taste of him, the thrill of his hands caressing her bare flesh and the memory would awaken a sweet ache deep inside.

Even now, thoughts of Steven dominated her exhausted mind.

Lenore set down the teacup and rested her head in her hands. Eyes closed, she rocked slowly, summoning past sorrows to battle her own traitorous emotions. Inside her the war raged, a ferocious struggle of love fighting to be freed, yet inevitably conquered by the most powerful, imprisoning grief.

To reinforce emotional survival, Lenore told herself that she didn't need a man to be complete. She was happy with her life and cherished her emotional independence. Perhaps Hettie had weakened but Lenore was young and strong, able to control her own destiny.

But in spite of such stoic resolve, Lenore drifted into a troubled sleep and dreamed of being swept away by a dark-haired man with forest-green eyes.

The creek was running clear and slow, its crystal waters swirling into lazy pools along a rocky bank. Lenore laughed and tiptoed across the fallen log bridging a narrow gully. Once on the other side, she waved, then called out in a voice that was half-teasing, half-taunting. "Come on, scaredy-cat. Are you afraid to get your feet wet?"

Steven stood on the far bank, staring at the log as though it were an assassin. His face was white, his expression grim. "I might fall."

"The water's shallow," Lenore insisted. "You won't be hurt."

Closing his eyes, he shook his head and looked away. "I don't want to do this."

"You have to follow me or you'll be lost forever," Lenore crooned in a sultry voice that was not her own. "You need me, Steven. Come to me. I'll show you the way. *Co-o-ome to me-e.*"

As though mesmerized, Steven turned and gazed across the widening creek. His eyes were blank as he walked to the log without blinking. Like a somnambulist, he stepped up and moved slowly across, looking neither right nor left, simply gazing into space as though being pulled by an unseen force.

Suddenly the creek exploded into a roaring river and as Lenore watched in horror, the log bridge stretched two hundred feet above a cataclysmic canyon.

"Stop!" Lenore cried but her warning came too late.

Steven reached out, whispered her name, then plummeted into the bottomless abyss while Lenore screamed over and over again, an agonized wail torn from the core of her tortured soul.

The image faded but the shrill noise continued, rousing Lenore from her troubled sleep. She bolted upright, heart pounding. Still terrified by the macabre nightmare, she was confused and unfocused, barely able to recognize that the telephone was ringing insistently.

Standing, she swayed slightly and stumbled across the room. She lifted the receiver and mumbled incoherently. A familiar voice echoed through the line and she nearly sobbed in relief. "Steven? Oh, thank God."

After a split-second pause, Steven's tone changed from brusque to anxious. "Are you all right?"

"Yes, yes. I'm fine." Shakily, she wiped her wet forehead and took a deep breath. Fully awake now, she noticed that the glaring sunlight was flooding in from the west. "What time is it?"

"You sound strange. Are you sure nothing is wrong?"

"No, really. I, ah, must have overslept."

His voice hardened again. "I guess you did. It's after three."

"In the afternoon?" Instantly Lenore was on her feet. Her first thought was the day-care center, then she realized that it was Saturday and moaned. Exhaustion had obviously fried her poor brain. Her fuzzy mind cleared slowly. "Where are you?"

"In my uncle's apartment."

His audible tension made Lenore edgy. "What is it, Steven? What's wrong?"

The line was silent a moment, then Steven spoke quietly. "They've eloped."

"Eloped? Who?" Lenore's stomach lurched and she absently clutched at her middle. "Oh, God no."

"I found the phone number of the Las Vegas Desert Inn on Edison's desk," Steven replied tiredly. "According to the manager, they drove off this morning with the entire complex throwing rice."

Because her knees couldn't support her, Lenore dropped heavily into a nearby chair and tried to gather her muddled thoughts. "There must be some mistake. Grandma would never get married without telling me."

"She did tell you. Last night. You weren't too happy about it, remember?"

A chill skittered down Lenore's spine. "Oh, Lord. I said such cruel things. I don't know what got into me. She must have felt so...betrayed. Oh, Steven, what are we going to do?"

"The next flight to Las Vegas leaves in two hours. I'll be on it."

"Book two seats," Lenore said instantly. "I'll meet you at the airport in thirty minutes."

After a brief pause, Steven spoke tightly. "Make it an hour. I have a stop to make first."

Dazed, Lenore listened to the dial tone for several seconds before cradling the receiver. Perhaps it didn't matter whether Hettie and Edison had years together or only weeks. Deep down, Lenore had always known that Edison made her grandmother happy but had conveniently ignored the unwelcome realization. Now she felt sick, realizing how deeply her accusatory attitude must have hurt Hettie.

Lenore was determined to make amends, to return that same unconditional love and support that her grandmother had always given so freely. She just prayed that it wasn't too late.

* * *

In the hotel's posh lobby, Steven and Lenore hogged the pay telephones and dialed frantically. With a disgusted sigh, Steven crossed the fifth all-night wedding chapel off his list. He had over a dozen more to call. Beside him, Lenore covered her ear in a fruitless attempt to drown out the clinking din of the nearby casino. After a moment, she hung up and looked at him.

"Nothing so far," she said, then added hopefully. "Maybe they changed their minds."

Steven responded with an ambivalent grunt. The guest book reflected only one hotel room registered in the name of Mr. and Mrs. Edison P. Collier. There was little point in mentioning that. Besides, he still held a faint hope that the optimistic supposition would prove accurate. Then there was the fact that Lenore suddenly seemed more concerned about attending the wedding than stopping it. That was definitely not what Steven had in mind. He was still grimly determined to keep Edison from making what would certainly be a disastrous mistake.

Steven, however, was nothing if not a realist. Although the prospect of preventing this foolish union had dimmed by the hour, he'd forseen and provided for that unpleasant possibility. In his breast pocket was a contingency plan, a carefully scripted nuptial agreement that his harried lawyer had drafted minutes before Steven boarded the Vegas-bound plane. One way or another, Steven intended to protect his uncle until the old devil came to his senses.

Steven stared into space mulling all aspects of this unhappy situation. Finally he realized that Lenore was eyeing him quizzically and he irritably dropped another quarter into the phone and dialed.

Over the next twenty minutes, Steven continued his thankless chore and slowly worked down the list. Wedding chapel number six was out of business. Number seven had recently performed a ceremony for an older couple but the woman had red hair and the man had been bald. Steven was repeating his practiced monologue on chapel number eight when Lenore suddenly grabbed his arm.

Her woeful expression spoke volumes and his heart sank like a rock. He hung up the phone and rubbed his forehead. "When?"

Lenore swallowed. "About an hour ago."

"Did they...?" He couldn't quite get the words out.

Her eyes were as big as saucers and she chewed her lower lip, as though trying not to cry. Finally she nodded and Steven swore softly. "Are you sure it was Hettie and Edison?"

"The chaplain read their names out of his book and described them perfectly." Lenore leaned against the wall beside the pay phone and avoided Steven's gaze. When she spoke again, her voice caught. "The chaplain's wife and sister-in-law acted as witnesses. The man said that he thought it...was sad that such a dear old couple had no one to stand up for them."

A tear slid down her face and Steven gently brushed it away. Her pitiful expression tore him up inside. He wanted to console her, to say something—anything—that would erase the misery in her eyes but he couldn't speak because his throat had suddenly constricted. Feeling helpless, he simply took her in his arms and held her until she stopped trembling.

Then Lenore took a shuddering breath and stepped back. "What should we do now?"

"Eventually they'll come back to the hotel. When they do, we'll be waiting."

Lenore nodded listlessly and allowed Steven to escort her to a private seating area in the far side of the lobby. He sat beside her and absently touched his jacket. At least the legal document offered an option to mitigate some portion of this unfortunate event. The thought offered surprisingly scant comfort.

After what seemed like a small eternity but was probably no more than thirty minutes, Lenore emitted a small gasp as Hettie and Edison strolled into the lobby. Smiling and radiant, the older couple were totally engrossed in each other and breezed past without a second glance.

"Grandma..." The single choked word was all Lenore could manage. It was enough.

Glancing back, Hettie's perplexed expression changed instantly to joy. Lenore hesitated then stumbled into her grandmother's waiting arms. The two women embraced, alternately laughing and wiping away discreet tears while Edison and Steven coughed, shifted uncomfortably and studied the lobby carpet.

Finally Lenore sniffed and stepped back. "I've crushed your lovely corsage."

"Think nothing of it, dear," Hettie crooned, brushing a strand of hair from Lenore's damp face.

"But it's your wedding bouquet..." Lenore's stoic expression crumpled with a fresh flood of tears. "Oh, Grandma, I'm so sorry for the terrible things I said—"

"Hush, child. I know how difficult this has been for you. I understand. But you're here now and that's all that matters, isn't it, Sonny?"

"Of course." Edison, who had been covertly judging Steven's reaction, managed a strained smile. "I'm glad you came, son."

That was Steven's cue and he knew it. Still, he nearly choked on the words. "Congratulations. I hope you'll both be very happy."

Edison's smile widened into a grin as he pumped Steven's hand. "We will be, son. Thank you. Now, let's all go kick up our heels and celebrate!"

"That's a wonderful idea," Hettie replied enthusiastically. "We'll have a sinfully fattening dinner and see one of those fancy shows and then we'll all go dancing until the sun comes up! Do you like slot machines, Lenore? I won two dollars in nickles... of course, it cost me four bucks but that's not the point, is it? Gracious, everything is so exciting—" Suddenly Hettie frowned and took Lenore's hand. "What's wrong, dear?"

Lenore licked her lips and plucked at the bodice of her limp cotton blouse. "I feel like we're intruding and besides, I'm not dressed for a night out."

"Nonsense! You just need to freshen up a bit, that's all. Lordy, wait until you see our beautiful room . . . all the tapestry and gorgeous antiques. Why, we even had a lovely basket of fruit compliments of the hotel. Have you ever heard of such a thing?" Grasping Lenore's elbow, Hettie propelled the startled young woman toward the elevator and called over her shoulder. "Hurry up, you two. We don't want to miss that dinner show."

Before Edison could comply, Steven laid a restraining hand on his uncle's shoulder. "Perhaps you'd allow me to buy you a drink, first." When Edison hesitated, Steven tightened his grip. "We have business to discuss."

The tension was thick enough to slice. Edison's smile evaporated and he offered a resigned nod. Across the lobby, Lenore plucked nervously at her sleeve while Hettie simply fixed Steven with a knowing stare. Finally the older woman smiled kindly then turned and chattering brightly, hustled Lenore into a waiting elevator.

After several seconds of unnerving silence, Steven ushered his uncle to the lounge adjoining the lobby. They found a quiet booth, ordered two beers, then stared silently at the shiny table until the waitress brought their drinks.

Steven took a healthy gulp of courage, then looked his uncle square in the eye. "Have you completely lost your mind?"

Showing no surprise at the brusque question, Edison simply sipped his beer and regarded Steven thoughtfully. Finally he set down the glass. "No, I don't think so. In fact, marrying Hettie is probably the smartest thing I've ever done. She's a wonderful woman."

Frustrated, Steven raked his hair and racked his brain trying to find the words to express his anxiety. Finally he blurted out a typical blunt statement. "Marriage is for fools."

"That's what I've always thought," Edison replied quietly. "And that's what I taught you. I was wrong."

"What if you weren't wrong?" Steven set his glass down so sharply that foam sloshed over the rim. "What if you end

p like my father, a hollowed-out shell of a man sucking
hiskey to numb the misery?"

Sadly shaking his head, Edison sighed and as though with
great effort, met Steven's angry gaze. "Your father lived
at way because he was too weak to do anything else." The
tartling comment took Steven's breath away but before he
ould gather his thoughts, Edison continued in a soft voice
at only shook a little. "Your mother and I never got
long, Steven. You knew that but you never really knew
hy, because I wouldn't admit the truth, even to myself.
ctually she wasn't a bad woman at all but I hated her
rength, her sense of purpose because it made your father
em even more pathetic by comparison. I couldn't blame
im because . . . well hell, he was my baby brother and I felt
sponsible for what he'd become."

Astounded by his uncle's intimate revelation, Steven
aned back and slowly exhaled stale air from his aching
ungs. In all the years he'd lived with Edison, he had never
eard his uncle exude such emotion. Edison had always been
ble to observe the world around him with dispassionate
bjectivity. Steven had admired his uncle's controlled
rength and had tried fruitlessly to emulate it. Had it all
een a ruse? Beneath the calm, stilted exterior, had Edison
een as unsure, as guilt-ridden as everyone else?

"I don't understand," Steven muttered, shaking his head
s though the sharp motion could clear his clouded mind.
How could you feel responsible for my father's drinking?
hat doesn't make any sense."

Edison shrugged. "My folks—your grandparents—didn't
ave a particularly happy marriage, either. Divorce wasn't
n option in those days, so they stayed together until both
f them just withered and died. I was still a kid myself, but
worked hard to raise my brother the best I could. He never
as a strong boy and I was always protecting him from one
ully or another. After he grew up, I wouldn't fight his bat-
es anymore and he went looking for someone who would."

"So he married my mother?"

"Seemed right to him, I suppose." Swirling his beer glass,
dison stared into the amber liquid as though it were a por-

tal to the past. "I watched my brother's life go down the toilet, same as our parents' had, and decided right then and there that the only way to avoid heartache was to avoid marriage. Work became my life."

That final sentence sent a chill down Steven's spine and he felt compelled to justify the philosophy that so closely paralleled his own. "Building a business from the ground up isn't a part-time job. You should be proud of your accomplishment. Hell, hard work and dedication isn't a crime."

"No, but I used work the same way your father used a bottle . . . as an escape."

"Escape from what?" Steven's voice rose and he suppressed an odd sense of panic. His uncle's speech had hit home, bruising some secret part of his own fallible soul.

Choosing his words with great care, Edison spoke with quiet dignity. "I was afraid to need anyone, afraid of the emotional risk. Fear and pain is natural, son, but when taken to the extreme, it becomes cowardice."

"That's ridiculous." Avoiding his uncle's gaze, Steven took a healthy swallow of beer. It did little to erase the bitter taste in his mouth and he grimaced, pushing the glass away. "So, when did you come to these startling philosophical conclusions?"

Edison shrugged. "When I got old. Suddenly I looked around and realized that I'd accomplished everything I ever thought important. I had money, freedom and the respect of those who, in the end, never really mattered. I could buy myself a big house and rattle around all alone, listening to the sound of my own footsteps. I had everything but I didn't really have anything at all."

The emotional disclosure was deeply touching. For the first time, Steven realized that although Edison could afford to spend his waning years in luxury, he'd selected the bustling retirement complex out of loneliness. The life-style Steven had so admired had actually been a solitary one, filled with people and activity, but no less empty and desolate. Steven had emulated his uncle's life only too well. All these years, he'd been as blind to Edison's inner torment as he'd been to his own.

Steven shook off the disquieting notion. This was not about him—it was about Edison and nothing changed the fact that a marriage based on desperation was ill conceived and quite obviously doomed.

Absently touching his breast pocket, Steven planned to produce the legal agreement but for some reason he didn't care to explore, couldn't bring himself to do so. At least, not yet. After a moment, he laid both hands on the table and took a deep breath. "So, you married Hettie strictly for companionship?"

Edison regarded his nephew sympathetically. "No, son. I married Hettie because I love her."

Steven stiffened. He could understand the loneliness. He could even understand the fear of growing old, but he couldn't quite accept that Edison was truly in love with Hettie. To do so would require Steven to accept his own emotional vulnerability and the fact that in some profound way, Lenore had touched it.

Steven wasn't ready to admit that yet. Perhaps he never would be.

"Are you sure you won't come to the midnight show with us, dear? My stars, the chance to see Engelbert Humperdinck in person doesn't come along every day."

Hettie's bright little eyes reflected major excitement but even if Lenore hadn't been completely wacked by the grueling day, she'd still have been hard-pressed to share her grandmother's enthusiasm for a sultry lounge crooner. "You and Edison go on now, and have a great time."

Hettie made a soft clicking sound. "First Steven pleads exhaustion and now you're pooping out on us. Young people nowadays don't seem to have any pep and vigor, isn't that right, Sonny?"

Standing in the doorway, Edison offered a lecherous grin. "If you're looking for vigor, my dear, I've got a surprise in store for you."

Blushing furiously, Hettie gave Edison's arms a playful punch, then hauled him away. Relieved to be alone, Lenore closed the door and glanced around the tiny room. It wasn't as grand as Hettie and Edison's suite, but then beggars can't be choosers. She felt fortunate that there were even two rooms available at such late notice.

Steven was right across the hall and Lenore toyed with the idea of calling him. Not that she had any deep-seated need to hear his voice, of course. She was concerned, that's all. Throughout the evening, Steven had been even moodier than usual. He hadn't spoken three words through dinner and during the floor show, he'd gazed into space with a lost expression that had a peculiar effect on Lenore's heart.

She flexed her fingers over the telephone receiver, then snatched her hand away. "He's probably asleep by now," she mumbled aloud and took comfort from the sound of her own voice. She talked to herself sometimes, when the silence was too loud.

Drawing a deep breath, she stared into the emptiness. "What you need, kiddo, is a hot shower and some serious shut-eye. Everything will seem different in the morning."

Different, perhaps, but not necessarily better. Something was eating her inside, something powerful yet undefinable. She ached. She throbbed with an infinite yearning that she secretly recognized but refused to acknowledge.

Absently rubbing her abdomen, she bit her lower lip and closed her eyes. She saw him in her mind, just as she'd known that she would. Steven. He was always there, his image floating just beyond reach.

There was a tentative knock on the door. Lenore's mouth went dry and her knees nearly buckled. It was him. Intuitively she knew that. She also knew that if she answered—if she opened that door and looked into those crystalline eyes—her life would be inexorably altered.

So why was her hand on the knob?

The wooden barrier magically swung open. Steven stood there, elbow propped against the jamb and hair endearingly mussed, looking agitated, bewildered and quite frankly, scared.

Unable to trust her voice, Lenore simply backed away to allow him access. He hesitated, then stepped in, reaching behind to push the door shut and seal out the world.

They were alone.

Lenore clasped her hands together to still her trembling fingers. Steven jammed his hands into his pockets and made production of studying the small room. Neither spoke.

After what seemed an eon of smothering silence, Lenore managed to stammer, "Hettie and Edison just left."

Since his hands were still tucked tightly away, Steven gestured toward the hallway with a nod. "I heard."

"Oh." The lame response was the best Lenore could manage.

Steven started to speak, cleared his throat, then tried again. "Are you okay?"

"Sure." Lenore wiped her damp hands together. "And you?"

He shrugged stiffly. "Yeah."

"Well, good. That's good."

"Right." He coughed and retrieved one hand to loosen his skinny tie. "I . . . should be going."

"I suppose so."

"It's late."

"Yes. Very late."

Lenore moved slowly toward him. He froze and held his breath. When she was close enough to feel the heat radiating from his body, she laid one hand on his chest and felt his heart race wildly. Another time, another place, Lenore might have considered the consequences of such boldness but at this moment, at this glorious moment, she was simply overcome by a desire to touch him. So she did.

She traced the sharp angle of his jaw, then allowed her fingertips to brush his strong mouth. A tiny muscle in his throat vibrated, an almost imperceptible quiver that revealed his potent desire. Craving more intimacy, Lenore awkwardly fumbled to unknot his tie, then tossed it to the floor without another thought.

Steven spoke in a strange, strangled voice. "Do you realize what you're doing?"

She ignored the choked question, mesmerized by another exciting discovery. Crisp dark hairs peeked through his open collar, tantalizing her. Slowly, methodically, she un-

buttoned his shirt until her palms tickled his bare skin. He
sucked in a sharp breath but allowed her to explore the hard
contours of his chest with her fingertips. She was enrap-
tured by his power and marveled at the smooth strength of
muscle straining toward her touch. Beneath the prickly mat
of hair, his skin was warm and slick, enticing her toward a
more intimate examination.

Suddenly Steven grabbed her wrist. Startled, she looked
up. "I don't like games," he warned softly. "When I play,
it's for keeps and I don't like to lose."

Before she could respond, his mouth was on hers, a deep
searching kiss that left her mind in shambles and her body
in shock. He tore his mouth away and took a ragged breath
before fixing her with a penetrating gaze. "Do you want me,
Lenore? Because I want you, honey, so much it's eating me
up inside but if you say the word, I'll walk out that door
right now."

Lenore licked her lips and whispered, "Don't go."

Steven closed his eyes, as though issuing a silent prayer
then looked at her with humbling reverence. With strokes
that seemed absurdly delicate for such strong hands, he ex-
plored her face and the subtle curve of her throat. She
emitted a small, deep whimper and tugged on his jacket with
increasing frustration.

Steven released Lenore long enough to shrug out of the
offending garment and it fell in a heap on the floor. That
accomplished, they clung to each other, lips and fingers
searching with frantic intensity. At the very moment that
Lenore felt she might die of such unrelenting passion, she
was vaguely aware that the jacket was tangled around her
feet. Distracted, she kicked it away and something fluttered
across the floor.

Lenore blinked, then tried to focus on the neatly folded
bound document. "Wh-what's that?"

"What?" Steven muttered, preoccupied with his quest to
relieve Lenore of her blouse.

"That." Strangely compelled, Lenore twisted from Steven's grasp and retrieved the odd paper. Her grandmother's name fairly leaped off the page. Stunned, Lenore

raightened and held the document as though it were con-
gious. "What . . . does this mean?"

Frowning, Steven rubbed his forehead and tried to fo-
us. "It doesn't mean anything."

After scanning the first sheet, Lenore felt faint. "Good
ord, this thing specifies in glorious detail that each and
very one of your uncle's assets to be retained as his sepa-
te and personal property."

Steven scratched his head. "It's just a standard nuptial
greement. There's nothing sinister here—"

"*Nothing sinister?*" Lenore shook the hateful papers.
You insult my grandmother's integrity, all but accusing her
f being some kind of gold digging black widow and all you
n say in your defense is that there's 'nothing sinister' go-
g on? My God, what kind of fool do you take me for?"

"What are you, nuts or something? The damned thing
n't even signed."

"Not yet but that's hardly the point, is it? Obviously you
dn't go to all this trouble for a pocket decoration. What
ppened, did Grandma throw it back in your face?"

"She hasn't seen it and neither has Edison." Steven laid
he palm on each side of his face and rolled his eyes in
ustration. "You're overreacting."

"Oh, am I?" Lenore was so furious that she couldn't even
e straight. "How dare you?"

"How dare I *what?*" Steven demanded, his own anger
sing. "How dare I consider my uncle's financial security?
ook, I'm not the bad guy here and if you would put your
ormones on hold for a minute, you might be able to tap
to some tiny pod of logic in that overwrought female brain
yours."

"That's the most pompous, chauvinistic statement I've
er heard."

"So because I won't heel like a drooling puppy every time
u snap your pink little fingers, now I'm a chauvinist.
ne." With two major-league stomps, Steven crossed the
om and snatched up his jacket. Straightening, he glared
her. "You know, a suspicious person might wonder about
ur violent reaction to a simple property rights agree-

ment. Could it be that you and your sweet old grand
mother had plans for my uncle's money after all?'' He
ducked as the offending document flew past his ear. ''Nice
pitch. I can see why you made the junior high all stars.''

''Damn you,'' Lenore whispered, blinking back tears.
''When I think how you suckered me, made me believe that
you weren't really a heartless cynic after all. I actually
thought you were a sensitive, loving man. What a joke. You
must have found my naiveté laughable.''

His expression softened. ''I never found you naive or
laughable.''

For a moment, she almost believed him. Almost. But she
couldn't allow herself to be drawn into his sweet web or
she'd be doomed to repeat the agony of the past. No one
was immortal. Even the most noble and enduring love could
be nothing more than a fleeting interlude, a single blink of
the eternal cosmic eye.

So Lenore couldn't let herself love Steven—she couldn't
risk another inconsolable loss. Squaring her shoulders, she
lifted her chin and spoke with chilling certainty. ''Get out.''

Her cold words had the desired effect. Lips thinned and
eyes flashing, Steven flipped the jacket across his shoulder.
''That's the best idea you've had all night.''

Then he walked out the door and out of her life.

Chapter Nine

Lenore tossed her purse on the table, flipped on the radio and issued a silent thanks for having survived another day. She'd only thought of Steven six or eight times today—a definite improvement.

After their heated exchange in Las Vegas, Lenore had immediately packed and caught the red-eye back to Los Angeles. The following morning, Lenore's phone call to Hettie had included an apology for the quick departure but her accompanying explanation had been less than complete. She hadn't told Hettie about the nuptial agreement.

Lenore was still questioning her motives for suppressing that vital information. She hadn't wanted to hurt her grandmother, of course, but deep inside Lenore also realized that Steven had been sincerely concerned about his uncle.

That didn't excuse his tacky methods. Lenore had repeatedly consoled herself that outrage had been perfectly justified and she was considerably better off without Steven Collier cluttering up her safe, orderly existence.

Now if she could just get him out of her mind . . .

The doorbell rang. Frowning, Lenore glanced at her watch and wondered who on earth would be calling so late in the evening. The bell jangled again and was followed by an insistent knock. Annoyed, Lenore walked quickly to the door and squinted through the peephole. "Grandma!"

Instantly Lenore whipped the door open and Hettie rushed inside, obviously agitated. "It's about time. A body could freeze to death waiting. Of course, most folks would croak out of pure exhaustion just trying to climb that cliff and get to your porch in the first place. Why don't you get yourself a nice place in the suburbs, dear? Then your poor old grandma won't need a pacemaker. Do you have any tea, child?"

Not waiting for an answer, Hettie tottered toward the kitchen.

Bewildered, Lenore dutifully followed. "When did you get back from Las Vegas?"

"Days ago...where's the kettle."

Lenore opened a lower cupboard and retrieved the requested item. "Why didn't you call me?"

"There was so much to do. Edison had given notice on his apartment some time ago so his things had to be moved to my place—I have a view of the pool, you know—then there were all kinds of boring details that had to be attended to. Change of address forms and banking business and hiring lawyers to handle our divorce—that kind of thing. Where's the sweetener, Lenore? You know I can't tolerate sugar."

Lenore stared dumbly. "Divorce?"

"Yes, dear." Hettie managed a too-bright smile. "Do you keep it in the pantry?"

"Keep what in the pantry?"

"The sweetener, of course. Never mind. I'll just take a look...ah. Here it is. How would you like your tea, dear?"

"I don't want any tea. Grandma, stop fussing with those cups and look at me." With an audible sniff, Hettie bit her lip and met Lenore's stunned gaze. "What is all this business about a divorce?"

Hettie blinked rapidly. "It's all over between Edison and me. The marriage was a terrible mistake. I . . . should have listened to you, Lenore. You were right."

"I don't understand," Lenore murmured. "You and Edison were so much in love . . . what happened?"

Hettie raised her plump chin, clasped her hands together and spoke with a quiver that nearly broke Lenore's heart. "I'll not live with a man who believes I'm after his money."

"Oh, God. The nuptial agreement." Lenore felt as if she'd swallowed a rock. "I can't believe that Edison actually asked you to sign that horrible thing."

"He didn't."

Lenore's heart sank even further. "Did Steven give it to you?"

"No one gave it to me."

"Then . . . I don't understand. How did you even know about it?"

Hettie sighed dramatically. "It's a long story, dear."

"I've got plenty of time." Lenore escorted her grandmother to the kitchen table and when both women were seated, she leaned over and fixed Hettie with a determined stare. "Now talk. Grandma, please, stop fidgeting and tell me what happened."

"All right, child. You needn't raise your voice." With a deep breath, Hettie pasted on a pained expression and launched into her plaintive tale. "After you called the hotel sounding like you'd lost your best friend, I was just worried sick, so Edison and I went to see if Steven knew anything. Well, he was packing to leave and didn't want to talk—he's even grumpier than his uncle, you know—but finally we pried the truth out of him. He admitted that you two had a big fat argument and then he told us what it was about. Well, you can imagine how I felt."

Reaching out, Lenore gave Hettie's hand a comforting squeeze. "You must have been terribly hurt."

"Yes, terribly." Hettie shuddered, as though the mere memory was too difficult to bear, and sneaked a covert glance to assess the extent of Lenore's empathy. Apparently satisfied, the older woman continued. "Steven apol-

ogized, of course. Said he meant no disrespect, but after he
left for L.A., Edison actually *defended* what he'd done. Can
you believe that? My own husband turned against me. Well,
the marriage was over right then and there, I can tell you."

"Wait a minute." Lenore rubbed her forehead and tried
to gather her thoughts. "Even though Edison didn't know
anything about the agreement, you're going to divorce him
anyway because he understood why Steven thought it was a
good idea?"

"Certainly. Why, if a man can't stand up for his wife, he's
not worth having, is he?"

Bewildered, Lenore could only stammer. "That doesn't
make any sense. Granted, Steven tends to be a bit overprotective and his manner is less than tactful, but you certainly
can't fault his motives. Edison wasn't being disloyal to you.
He was simply trying to explain things from Steven's perspective."

After staring silently into her lap, Hettie slanted another
sly glance then went in for the kill. "Your grandfather would
never have tolerated such an attack on my honor."

Lenore sat upright and stared. "Grandpa was the mel-
lowest, most rational man I've ever known. I seriously
doubt that he would have considered Edison's behavior to
be out of line."

"Perhaps not, but...I don't think he'd approve of
Sonny."

"Grandpa would want you to be happy," Lenore insisted and was shocked to realize that she actually believed
that. "If you and Edison truly love each other, then a stupid piece of paper isn't worth the disintegration of a beautiful relationship."

After considering Lenore's words, Hettie's shoulders
heaved helplessly. "It's too late now. Edison's moving out
today and that's the end of it."

"Oh, Grandma—"

"No sense crying over spilled milk," Hettie interrupted
brightly. "What's done is done. Life goes on, you know."

With that final pronouncement, Hettie made a production out of tearing open the tiny packet of sweetener and

tirring her tea until Lenore wondered if the spoon would dissolve.

Unable to stand the sight of her grandmother's wounded expression, Lenore stood and walked to the far side of the kitchen. She slumped over the counter, riddled by guilt. This had been her fault, after all. She'd been so myopic, so unreasonably determined to keep Hettie and Edison apart that he'd succeeded beyond her wildest dreams. But there was no triumph in this tragedy and Lenore fervidly sought some way to repair the damage she'd caused.

"What if I talked to Edison?" Lenore mused aloud. "Maybe I could explain everything—"

"There's nothing to explain," Hettie interrupted. "He's made his decision and I'll not be begging him to come back, after all. Even old women have their pride, you know."

Helplessly Lenore turned and extended her palm in a pleading gesture. "Isn't there anything I can do?"

"Well, there *is* one small thing."

"Name it," Lenore replied quickly, too distraught to note the crafty gleam in her grandmother's eye. "I'll do anything you want."

"Wonderful!" Hettie chortled, clasping her hands below her chin. "How soon can you be packed, dear? Bring swimsuits, skimpy two-piece jobs, mind you, not those awful old-lady coverups . . . and you do have a few sexy sundresses, don't you? If not, we'll simply have to go shopping. We can't take Cabo San Lucas by storm if you dress like a nun on holiday."

"Cabo San— Wait a minute. That's in Mexico, isn't it?"

"Umm. Baja, actually, right on the tip of the peninsula. Lovely place. Very romantic." Pausing long enough to regard Lenore with a critical eye, Hettie frowned and rubbed her fat little chin. "Perhaps we should have your hair done. Curls, perhaps, something with a little pizzazz."

"Pizzazz?" Absently Lenore touched her hair then snatched her hand away. "Wait just a minute. What's going on here?"

Hettie seemed surprised by the question. "Why, we're making plans, dear."

"Plans for what?"

With exaggerated patience, Hettie explained. "Our trip to Cabo San Lucas, of course. The flight leaves at noon tomorrow so we really haven't much time to prepare."

Astounded and outmaneuvered, Lenore could barely squeak out a protest. "I can't go anywhere tomorrow."

"Certainly you can. Jackie and Maggie have agreed to cover for you at the center so we're as free as birds for the next week." Hettie cheerfully bustled to the sink and rinsed out the teacups. "The reservations are all made and everything has been paid for. It would be a shame to waste such lovely honeymoon plans simply because the marriage didn't work out. Besides, you and I will have a marvelous time. Why, I feel better already."

"Grandma, really, I can't—" The words stuck in Lenore's throat.

"What can't you do, child?" Hettie asked, anxiously wringing a damp dishrag.

"I . . . can't wait."

As Hettie's round face split into a dazzling grin, Lenore emitted a resigned sigh and gracefully accepted defeat. If it made her grandmother happy, a few days on a Baja beach was a small sacrifice.

Steven slammed around the galley searching for something edible. He wasn't really hungry but his stomach was. What Steven really craved was chicken soup out of a thermos, lovingly served by the dimpled, dark-haired woman that haunted every waking moment.

"Damn!" Frustration exploded and he swiped his arm angrily over the tiny counter. Dishes crashed to the floor and Steven couldn't have cared less. He was furious with himself and with the woman who had exposed his weakness.

From the deck outside, Butch barked frantically.

"Quiet!" Steven growled irritably. The last thing he needed right now was a ration of canine back talk. But unmoved by his master's foul humor, the animal continued to yip annoyingly. Finally Steven could handle no more. "Get in here!" His stern command was rewarded by silence and a squeak on the cabin stairs. "Good boy," Steven mumbled, staring out the galley porthole. "Now go lay down."

"If you don't mind, son, I'd rather just sit."

Startled, Steven whirled so quickly that his head smacked a cabinet. Grabbing his throbbing skull, he cursed and squinted toward the doorway. There stood Edison, suitcase in hand, looking as wretched as Steven felt. "What in hell—?"

Edison interrupted politely. "Will my bag be in the way here?"

"Ah, no... of course not." Wincing, Steven gingerly touched the swelling lump on his scalp and saw Butch peering cautiously into the cabin. After a moment, the animal backed away and his tapping toenails crossed the deck. Steven skeptically eyed his uncle. "What's going on?"

After pushing his luggage under the dinette table, Edison sat hunched on the sofa. "Hettie left me," he said bleakly.

The statement didn't really sink in. "Left you where?"

Edison twitched his mustache and spread his hands with dramatic flair. "It's over. Kaput. Finished."

"What's over?"

Exasperated, Edison glared up. "That bop on the head must have scrambled your brains. Dadgum it, Steven, I'm trying to tell you that Hettie and I have split up. The least you can do is pretend to be interested."

That got Steven's attention. "Split up? You've got to be joking. Good Lord, you haven't been married a week. I don't believe this... you're putting me on, right?"

Satisfied by his nephew's belated reaction, Edison leaned back and replaced his vexed expression with one more suitable to abject misery. "It's the gospel truth, son, sad as it is. I should have listened to you in the first place. Say, you wouldn't happen to have a nip of good bourbon around, would you?"

"Bourbon? Well, I might have a pint— Now wait a minute. You don't drink hard stuff."

"I don't? Hmm." Edison shrugged one furry white eyebrow. "Then it's high time I started. Make it a double."

Steven hesitated, then figured what the hell. He located two unbroken glasses and filled each with a healthy dollop of hundred proof. "Here. Now would you please tell me what on earth is going on?"

Edison took the offered glass and studied the contents meticulously. "This stuff looks potent."

"It is. Look, Edison—"

"Phewww." Edison screwed up his nose and made a gagging sound. "It smells like kerosene."

Frustrated, Steven gulped half his own drink in a single swallow, coughed twice, wheezed once, then managed to croak. "There. I'm not trying to poison you so will you kindly tell me *what in hell is happening?*"

Edison blinked, appearing stung by Steven's tone. "You don't have to yell."

Sighing, Steven sat tiredly beside his uncle. "I'm sorry."

Mollified, Edison balanced his glass on one knee and leaned back. "It all started with that nuptial agreement. Hettie was very upset, you know."

Steven grimaced. "I'll talk to her, explain that you had nothing to do with it."

"You'll do no such thing! Why, you had every right to have that document drawn up. If I'd been in my right mind, I would have seen to it myself."

Steven rubbed his ear. "Excuse me?"

"A man can't be too careful, especially at my age. There's no time to make up for mistakes, don't you agree?"

"Well, sure. I mean, I guess so, but—"

"No buts about it. You were right and that's just what I told Hettie."

Moaning, Steven rubbed his knuckles over his eyelids and tried to clarify what his uncle had said. "Let me see if I understand this. Did you actually ask Hettie to sign that agreement?"

"Not exactly." Edison's interest in bourbon returned suddenly and he took a healthy swallow. "Go-o-od Lor-r-rd," he rasped, fanning his mouth wildly. *"Water!"*

"It's in the tap," Steven replied brusquely, ignoring the fact that his uncle had already dashed to the sink and was

llowing the faucet to run into his open mouth. "What 'ex-
ctly' *did* you ask her to do?"

Panting, Edison dried his mustache with the back of his
and. "Nothing."

"Oh, come on. Hettie's a bright, intelligent woman. She's
ot the type to walk out because you did absolutely noth-
g."

"Why Steven, I'm shocked. Are you taking her side?"

"I'm not taking anybody's side. I don't even know what's
oing on here! A few days ago, you were swooning in love
ith the woman. *What happened?*"

Edison's lips tightened stubbornly. "Maybe I just wanted
o be in love because I looked in the mirror and suddenly
w an old fool with white whiskers and hairy ears staring
ack at me. So maybe I got scared and held on to the first
oman who'd have me."

Unconvinced, Steven frowned.

Edison angled a stealthy glance at his brooding nephew,
en emitted a theatrical sigh. "Woman flat aren't worth the
rief, are they? Isn't that what you've been trying to tell me
ll this time?"

"Well, yes, but that doesn't mean I was right."

"Of course you were right! And it runs in the family, too.
ake Lenore, for instance."

Steven's head snapped up and his eyes flashed a warn-
g. "What about Lenore?"

Edison rubbed his hands together. "Look how shabbily
e treated you, running off that way."

Criticism of Lenore hit Steven deep in his gut and he sup-
ressed a surge of indignation. "She had good reason to be
ngry. I insulted her grandmother."

Waving away that rationale, Edison continued blithely
n. "Nonsense. She's just hysterical, like every other
oman in the world. Hormones, you know."

"Now wait just a damn minute—"

"Don't get me wrong. She's a lovely girl and I'll bet she's
real tiger . . . you know . . . in the romantic sense."

Steven balled his fists and clenched his teeth. "Don't say
nother word."

"I didn't mean anything," Edison replied innocently, blue eyes gleaming.

Nerves on edge, Steven replied with an angry grunt and took another swig of bourbon. The liquid stung his throat and made his eyes water. After a moment, a tingling warmth spread through his extremities and the tension seeped slowly away. He was fuzzily aware that Edison was grinning rather strangely for a man on the brink of emotional collapse, but Steven was too engrossed with his own odd reactions to pay much attention.

Edison's crude reference to Lenore had sent Steven's blood pressure soaring and he didn't quite know why. The woman wasn't a saint, after all, and Steven was well aware of her faults. But that didn't give anyone else, even his beloved uncle, the right to criticize her. Where Lenore was concerned, Steven felt protective and possessive, unnerving emotions that were new to him. He didn't much care for the feeling.

Suddenly he was anxious for distraction. He took another drink and regarded his uncle. "So what now?"

"Umm?" Instantly Edison replaced the stupid grin with a somber expression. "Well, son, I'd hoped you would let me stay here for a while."

Steven sat up. "What's wrong with your place?"

With exaggerated effort, Edison hoisted his suitcase to the dinette table and fumbled with the zipper. "Like a damn fool, I let Hettie talk me into moving in with her. They rented my beautiful apartment in less than two days. May I put my shaving supplies in the head?"

Slumping back, Steven managed a weak nod. He loved his uncle but had always considered his privacy to be inviolable. Still, the situation would only be temporary. He hoped.

Scooping up his razor and assorted bottles, Edison disappeared into the tiny commode area, chatting happily. "Hell, this will be like old times, won't it? Remember all those wonderful weekends we shared when you were a boy? Those were the days, weren't they? Nothing to think about except keeping the hooks baited and wondering if the weather would hold." Edison emerged and began rooting rough his luggage. "Yes, indeed, just like old times, only now I'll be the one sleeping on the bench cushions."

Steven watched glumly. "You can have the bedroom."

"Wouldn't hear of it. After all, this is your home." Edison gazed around the compact interior with obvious distaste and muttered, "Such as it is. I mean, it's fine for weekend recreation but— Never mind."

Curiosity piqued, Steven leaned forward. "But what?"

"It's not important." When Steven shrugged and gazed at the window, Edison continued anyway. "I was just going to say that most young men would be looking forward future expansion. You know, room for the wife and kids, at sort of thing. Of course, you're not interested in having a family."

"No, I'm not," Steven pronounced firmly.

"Good for you."

Edison whistled a sea-faring tune and refolded his underwear while Steven squirmed. The liquor hadn't dimmed his brain so much that he wasn't aware that Edison's cheerfulness didn't quite fit the broken-hearted scenario. Before could mull that further, Edison suddenly whirled and snapped his bony fingers.

"Say, I've got a great idea. Why don't we take off for a few days and do some fishing."

"I don't th—"

"We could cruise down the coast, kick back and relax. I hear the yellowtail are biting down south... remember the last time we went after yellowtail?" Edison chuckled to himself. "You caught this fish that was bigger than you were and fought him for nearly an hour. When the line broke, you were so spitting mad that you nearly dumped the entire right into the ocean."

Steven smiled, recalling those happier times. "I remember. It cost me six months' profit from my paper route to pay for that rod and reel."

"So how about it?" Edison urged. "First thing tomorrow, shall we cast off and set course for sunshine and blue waters?"

After a moment's hesitation, Steven met his uncle's anxious gaze. "Sure, why not?"

Edison beamed. Standing, Steven stretched lazily, surprised to realize that he was actually looking forward to the trip. It might get his mind off Lenore. He doubted it, but hope springs eternal. "I'd better check in at the job site tonight and let the foreman know what's going on."

Since it was nearly dusk, Edison was surprised. "Why the crew working on double shift?"

"We're trying to meet schedule on the parking structure. The architect insists that this new design can support three layers of iron with fewer weight-bearing columns to clutter up the parking floors."

Edison was skeptical. "That's new to me."

"I know. Supposedly it's the wave of the future." Steven lifted his leather jacket from a nearby hook. "Actually I'm not totally sold myself. The theory sounds great but construction a bit dicier because the side beams have to be braced six ways from Sunday while the iron is laid. Anyway, I should be back by ten."

"Take your time, son. By the time you get back, the *Bohemian* will be provisioned and ready to go."

"Great. See you later." Steven paused on the first step and glanced over his shoulder. "By the way, you never said exactly where we're going."

"Oh, I thought we might cruise down the Baja peninsula toward Cabo San Lucas." Edison's blue eyes twinkled. "Trust me, son, this will be one trip you'll never forget."

At night the construction site was lit like an amusement park, with each massive machine decorated by halogen wreaths. Down in the chilly open basement, Steven glanced up through the ribbon of rafters and was blinded by the glaring spotlights aimed directly into the pit. Beside him, the foreman studied each brace and bolt, then scrawled notes on a clipboard.

"Have all the braces been secured?" Steven asked.

"Everything is in place and going according to plan." The foreman squinted up. "The middle sure as hell looks empty without those extra columns."

Steven knew exactly what he meant. He, too, was uncomfortable but the city's most prestigious architectural firm had designed every truss and joist, and the plan had been blessed by everyone from the city building department to the state architectural review board. Steven had even checked the mathematics himself. Everything fit. The footings would hold, or so it said in the design manual.

Still, the nervous foreman was right. The place *did* look empty and the shell seemed unnervingly fragile.

Glancing up, Steven saw Chester the crew chief sauntering toward them. When the blocky little man arrived Steven sighed. "What's wrong now?"

Chester grimaced, scratched and gazed upward. "Crane's got more problems."

Steven looked up. The machine's immense arm extended over the pit with a two-ton beam dangling from its giant jaw. "What kind of problems?"

"Don't rightly know. Transmission, maybe. Can't seem to push her into reverse."

Steven's jaw twitched. The machine couldn't be moved from its precarious perch and that spelled trouble. He didn't like this one damn bit. If that beam dropped—

"Clear the floor," Steven snapped. "Get those iron workers down. Pull everyone out until—"

A horrible squeal drowned out Steven's words. He swore and saw the crane listing dangerously. Unbalanced, the beam swayed and the movement caused the arm to lurch violently.

"Oh, God," the foreman whispered.

"This ain't good," Chester pronounced, rubbing his whiskered chin.

Without thought, Steven pushed both men backward and screamed over the deafening roar. "Move! Now!"

A moment later, the concrete basement was filled with twisted iron rubble.

* * *

Lenore neatly folded a blouse and tucked it into her suitcase. She had little enthusiasm for this trip but couldn't back
out now. Although Lenore was well aware of Hettie's blatant manipulation, she wasn't particularly upset. If the circumstances warranted, Hettie had absolutely no qualms
about implementing whatever behavior, devious or not, that
the situation required. It was frequently frustrating, of
course, but Grandma's brain simply worked that way and
Lenore loved her anyway.

Besides Lenore suspected that Hettie's stiff-upper-lip attitude on the impending divorce was all an act. She didn't
have a doubt in the world that her grandmother truly loved
Edison. Even Hettie, with her flair for the dramatic,
couldn't have faked her radiant glow whenever Edison was
nearby.

The entire situation was just so pitiful.

Lenore sat on the bed and pondered the perplexities of
life. Less than two weeks ago, she'd been plotting ways to
extricate Hettie from Edison Collier's lecherous clutches.
Now she was desperately searching for a miracle to bring
them back together.

"Be careful what you wish for," she mumbled aloud and
instantly her thoughts turned to Steven. What was he doing
now? she wondered. Did he ever think about her?

With a disgusted groan, Lenore stood and paced the carpeted bedroom. Of course he didn't think about her. He'd
made his feelings quite clear. Why couldn't she accept that?

Because . . . she just couldn't.

And that infuriated her. She didn't want to think about
Steven Collier anymore. She didn't want his handsome image invading her sleep and she absolutely hated the way her
chest constricted every time she heard his name.

Muttering to herself, she flipped on the television to
drown out the sound of her own thoughts and concentrate
on the task of packing her suitcase. Maybe Hettie had been
right. They both needed to get away for a while. White sand,
blue water, tanned men . . . all right, scratch the tanned men,
but it'll still be great. Right?

"Right." She slammed the suitcase shut and snapped the fasteners. Behind her the television blared with a dog food commercial and Lenore instantly pictured Butch. She smiled. He was a nifty animal, kind of laid-back but with intelligent black eyes that seemed almost human. She missed Butch. She missed Steven.

Lenore threw up her hands. "Oh, Lord, I'm absolutely hopeless."

The commercial ended. Lenore whirled, planning to turn off the stupid television and soak in a hot tub until she'd steamed herself pink. Her hand was on the knob when an oddly familiar scene flashed on the screen. It took a moment for her to realize that she was watching a special news report on some kind of local disaster.

The newscaster's voice droned. "...Number of casualties are unknown but witnesses state that at least a dozen men were on site at the time of the collapse."

Lenore's lungs deflated and she clutched at her throat. That's why the video seemed so familiar. She was sitting here, her heart in her mouth, staring at the smoking ruins of Steven's construction site.

"Oh, no," she whispered. "God, no. Not again. Not Steven."

The grisly news report continued. "Two are known dead and firefighters believe that as many as six men may be trapped in the rubble."

Panic exploded like a bomb and Lenore leaped to her feet, screaming at the hateful screen. Grabbing her head, she tried desperately to concentrate. Her car keys. Dear God, where were her car keys?

She tore through the house, flinging books and vases to the floor, ignoring the tinkling of cracked glass, cognizant of one driving thought—she had to find Steven.

If she lost him now, he'd never know the truth. He'd never know how much she loved him.

Chapter Ten

In a state of raw panic, Lenore drove wildly to the construction site. She screeched into the cordoned parking area and faced the hideous incarnation of her worst nightmare. A dozen emergency vehicles obstructed her view, their eerie lights strobing the muggy blackness like garish balefires. The scene was permeated by the vicious stench of terror that was a morbid déjà vu of the horror that had haunted her for six long years.

Almost hysterical by now, Lenore's shaking fingers struggled with the lever. When the car door finally swung open, she didn't bother to close it and dashed into the chaos. This time, no one tried to stop her.

A harried policeman gestured toward another arriving ambulance. Lenore grabbed his arm and yanked furiously. "Steven Collier," she croaked.

"Move back, lady," the officer growled.

"Please..."

Pushing her aside with one arm, the policeman directed the emergency vehicle through the crowd, then wiped his forehead and returned his attention to Lenore. "Are you a relative?"

She didn't hesitate. "Yes. Please, can you help me?"

"Check with the guy in the plaid shirt." A popping flashbulb distracted him and the officer quickly headed toward the offending photographer.

Whirling, Lenore scanned the mob scene for a man in plaid. She pushed through a milling group of sullen construction workers, asked about Steven and received a disappointing assortment of bewildered shrugs.

Then Lenore stumbled up an uneven embankment toward the area where rescuers were hoisting something out of the rubble. When she reached the crest, she pressed her knuckles against her mouth to keep from screaming. Fully one third of the parking structure had collapsed into a twisted tangle of iron and steel.

Dear God, no one could have survived that. No one.

A huge crane was tilted into the mess, wedged between the basement's concrete foundation and one of the few bracing beams still intact. Beside the trapped machine, a half-dozen men worked feverishly to guide a winched cable up from the bowels of the wreckage. Lenore watched in horror as a litter emerged, dangling critically in midair before frantic workers hauled it to safety. A bloodied body was strapped to the carrier.

With a strangled cry, Lenore lurched toward the prostrate form. Paramedics instantly surrounded the injured man, barking orders and attaching a frightening array of medical devices to his poor battered body. Lenore choked back a sob when she recognized him. Her knees buckled and she dropped to the lumpy ground.

It wasn't Steven.

Tied to the stretcher basket was the rude little worker who had hollered at her for wandering too close to the excavation. But recognition offered no relief. The squat, square-faced man was obviously hurt, but at least he was alive. She had no such assurance about Steven's fate.

As the crew carried the stretcher to a waiting ambulance, Lenore finally spotted the elusive man in plaid, engrossed in studying a clipboard and conferring with one of the rescuers. All she could see was his back but he was tall and had broad shoulders and tufts of dark hair were sticking out from beneath a yellow hard hat. Her heart leaped hopefully.

Struggling to her feet, she ran toward him. "Steven!" The man didn't turn until she tripped against him, trembling and gasping for breath. She clutched his sleeve. "Stev...?"

The man steadied her. "Are you all right, miss?"

Numbly Lenore stepped back and fought tears, pulling away from the stranger's concerned grasp. Her lungs were ready to burst and the ground was spinning strangely. She was vaguely aware that someone had hold of her shoulders but she ignored the warm pressure and concentrated on salvaging a shred of rational thought.

Maybe she hadn't been able to find Steven because he wasn't even here. That had to be it. Steven had probably gone home long before the accident had even occurred. She was worrying about nothing. Everything was all right. It had to be.

"Miss? Do you need a doctor?"

The kind voice seemed far away and Lenore felt oddly detached from the grim surroundings. When the distant question was repeated, she managed a weak response. "No. I'm all right."

"Then you'll have to leave the area."

"Steven Collier," she blurted. "Do you know him?" The man's hand dropped from her shoulder and his expression tightened. Lenore's words rushed more quickly. "Has he been here tonight? I mean, Steven should be told about this, shouldn't he? Someone should call him—" The rambling sentence died on her lips as he avoided her gaze. "What...is it? Please, you know something. Tell me. Dear God, *tell me!*"

Without flinching, the man in plaid captured Lenore's flailing wrists. "Steven was in the area at the time of the collapse," he said gently.

She stiffened. "Where is he now?"

Instead of answering, he gestured to a nearby worker. "Take this lady over to rescue control and stay with her."

Lenore yanked away, eyes rounded in horror. "He's...
down there, isn't he? Steven's down in that godforsaken
hole, *isn't he?*"

After prying her frantic fingers from his shirt, the man
turned away but not before Lenore saw the bitter truth in his
eyes. Steven was trapped beneath tons of torn metal. He
could be hurt, he could be dying, and there wasn't one
damned thing Lenore, or anyone else, could do.

Then she fainted.

He was aware only of blackness and thought heaven must
be a disappointingly drab place.

Slowly, painfully, Steven's thoughts focused. He remembered the deafening noise and the choking dust clogging his
lungs. He remembered the earth rumbling beneath his feet
and the bruising rain of debris. And a moment before he'd
passed out, he remembered calling Lenore's name.

Now he heard a soft groan and realized that the sound
had come from him. But he felt no pain and vaguely
thought it odd that he'd be moaning when he couldn't feel
anything. Under the circumstances, he didn't consider that
a blessing. Was he paralyzed? Worse, was he actually dead?
No, he couldn't be dead because his brain still worked.

But then who could say that the mind ceased simply because the body expired? This was all too bizarre.

From somewhere above, Steven was vaguely aware of
droning machinery. Gradually he realized that he could not
only hear, but he could actually feel a faint vibration. That
was definitely a good sign. At least part of his nervous system was still functioning.

Steven also realized that his head hurt like hell and something sticky was dripping into his eyes. The sensation wasn't
comfortable but the message was encouraging.

Now if only he could move his arms—

Pain exploded from elbow to shoulder with enough force
to strangle his agonized scream. When the spasm subsided,
Steven groggily recognized that his right arm was pinned
beneath a jagged hunk of broken concrete. Well, at least he
wasn't paralyzed.

Testing his left arm, he felt around his black prison. His fingers grazed ragged barbs of twisted rebar and a length of iron beam angling upward. The corrugated steel that had been temporary flooring on the structure's upper levels had apparently caved in, cocooning the small crawl space in which he was trapped. That had probably saved his life but it also concealed him from the rescue operation he knew must be in full swing by now.

From his awkward position, Steven groped his tiny enclosure and realized that had his arm not been pinned, he probably had enough room to stand and walk around.

Still, he could see nothing and gingerly touched his eyelids, assuring himself that they were indeed open. So, he was either blind or there wasn't so much as a peephole in this twisted tomb.

Thinking more clearly now, Steven remembered pushing away Chester and the foreman right before the collapse. Perhaps they were nearby. He called out. Silence answered. Again and again he shouted futilely and felt sick. He prayed that the two men had managed to get beyond the falling girders but secretly doubted they'd been able to escape. Everything had happened too fast.

Judging by the thrumming engines, the rescue effort was some distance away. It would be hours before they reached him. Maybe days. He idly wondered if he would last that long. He didn't know how badly he was bleeding, nor could he ascertain whether anything besides his wrist was broken, but after a brief physical inventory, he decided he wasn't too badly injured. As long as he had air to breathe, Steven was determined to hang on. He had to.

Death wasn't the most frightening part of this ordeal. Steven didn't want to die but if his number was up, he could cope with that. But if he died tonight, he'd never see Lenore again.

And that's what really terrified him.

Eyes glazed, Lenore slumped forward and hugged her knees. She sat on the ground in a far corner of a command control center that consisted of several circled vehicles and a throng of grim uniformed personnel. Portable tables had been scattered haphazardly to support various communication devices and coffee supplies for exhausted workers. From her vantage point Lenore could watch the rescuers' progress and since the area was off limits to the gaggle of reporters beyond the ribboned perimeter, she had some protection from the indignity of having cameras recording her private agony.

Throughout the tortuous ordeal, Lenore was surrounded by the sights and the sounds and the sickening smell of death, a grisly replay of the night she'd lost Michael. Now Steven's life flickered on the brink of extinction. It was too much to bear. If she lost Steven, his final memory would be of cruel words and bitterness, just as Michael's had been.

In spite of the tearing guilt, Lenore recognized that at least Michael had known that he'd been loved. Steven had no such consolation.

Over the years Lenore had been offered many chances for love but had been too cowardly to accept such a precious gift. Because she had been so desperately afraid of loss, she'd put up an impenetrable wall against that, which gave purpose to life. Without love, one was doomed to merely exist in the drudgery of days without joy and nights without solace. That would be Lenore's hell, an earthly purgatory of regret and despair.

"Lenore! Oh, Lordy child, what are you doing here?"

Dazed, Lenore stood shakily and stared blankly toward the familiar voice. Hettie appeared like a specter and enveloped Lenore in a surprisingly solid embrace. The soothing scent of lilacs surrounded her and she clung to her grandmother's soft bulk, fighting a new rush of tears.

Hettie gently patted Lenore. "There, there, dear. Everything will be all right."

Finally Lenore hiccuped and stepped away from the consoling warmth. "Did you hear about the accident on the news?"

"News? Gracious, no, dear. I was so pooped from packing that I was in bed by nine." Hettie attempted a light tone but her plump face was lined with tension and she wrung her hands anxiously. She glanced over her shoulder then looked quickly back and launched into an extended explanation. "The phone woke me up. It was someone looking for Sonny and I guess he'd gotten that recorded message—you know, the one that says a telephone number had been changed to such and such? Anyway, Sonny is still an official emergency contact for Collier Development and this fellow was really quite adamant and I knew Sonny would want to be here so I rushed right over to the dock and picked him up." Hettie took a fast breath. "Do you know anything else, dear? About Steven, I mean?"

"No...they haven't found him yet." Lenore's head was swimming. Ordinarily she would have been instantly intrigued by the startling news that Sonny had been staying on Steven's boat and the fact that her grandmother had been so well informed on her soon-to-be-ex-husband's whereabouts. At the moment, however, Lenore was too stressed and exhausted to notice the inconsistency.

When Hettie again glanced expectantly over her shoulder, Lenore followed her gaze and saw Edison engaged in serious conversation with a group of emergency service personnel. Lenore bit her lip, praying that the news wasn't as bleak as the older man's expression indicated. After a moment, Edison nodded brusquely and walked toward the waiting women.

When he arrived, Hettie silently laid a hand on his sleeve, then they both stared somberly at Lenore. Meeting Edison's tired gaze, she was instantly chilled to the bone. The older man's eyes, glazed by sorrow and despair, revealed the depth of his torment. Instinctively Lenore realized that Edison didn't believe that Steven was alive.

"No," Lenore whispered, unable to accept the ghastly prognosis. "They'll bring him out. He'll be all right...he has to be, don't you understand? Nothing will happen to Steven. Fate couldn't be that cruel. My God, Edison, what would we do without him? I couldn't bear it, I just.. couldn't..."

Edison emitted a strangled gasp and gathered Lenore in his lean arms. "Steven will be just fine," he mumbled without conviction. "Everything will work out, you'll see."

Sniffling, Lenore pulled away and nodded vigorously. "Of course it will."

Avoiding her gaze, Edison cleared his throat and swallowed with some difficulty. When he again looked toward Lenore, he'd regained his composure. "There's nothing you can do here," he said kindly. "Your grandmother will take you home. You rest. I'll call when . . . Steven is rescued."

Lenore's chin raised automatically. "I'm not leaving."

Hettie stepped forward, clasping her chubby hands. "You're exhausted, dear. Sonny is right, there's nothing either of us can do and we're just in the way here." When Lenore stubbornly folded her arms, Hettie emitted a resigned sigh. "All right, then. We'll all stay."

And so they stood and watched, each suppressing helpless panic and portraying feigned confidence for the sake of the others, until dawn's gray pall gave birth to a new day.

It was getting harder to breathe.

Because movement caused excruciating pain, Steven had settled on a clumsy, bent-forward position that alleviated some pressure on his trapped arm but made his tortured lungs battle for every gasping breath. He'd dismissed the chilling thought that he might be depleting a limited oxygen supply. The absolute blackness and stale atmosphere was disconcerting but Steven thought it highly unlikely that the imprisoning wreckage had been compacted into an airtight mass. Unlikely, but not impossible.

The unpleasant prospect caused his heart to beat faster, using up even more precious oxygen. Panting, Steven adjusted his legs and rested his head on his knees. He struggled to envision a soothing image—waves breaking on white sand, palm trees swaying in a warm breeze—anything that would ease his suffering and slow his frantic pulse.

The pain was sudden, impaling him like a white-hot blade. Steven groaned, gritting his teeth and holding his breath until the agony subsided, then he exhaled carefully.

Apparently waves and palm trees weren't the answer.

Every muscle in his body protested the enforced abuse. His chest was constricted and his trapped arm throbbed relentlessly. Liquid fire coursed through his veins and something sharp and cruel was mercilessly battering the inside of his skull.

Disoriented by the pain, Steven squeezed his eyelids together and fuzzily wondered if he was upside down or right side up. Of course, he wasn't sure which side was his right side... or wrong side. Did people have a wrong side? Probably but it didn't matter.

What didn't matter? What had he just been thinking about? Had he even been thinking at all? Even his thoughts made no sense anymore.

Lenore.

Her image flooded his mind like a heavenly light. She was smiling, eyes twinkling in rainbow hues and that one crazy dimple sparkling just about the corner of her lush mouth.

Steven absently smiled back at her.

She laughed then and he actually heard the delightful, bell-like chuckle as clearly as if she'd been seated beside him. Her hair was so shiny, a cap of silky sable framing her sturdy, snub-nosed face. He was enveloped in her essence, surrounded by her sweet, sensual fragrance. She was with him.

A calming warmth washed over his body, easing his cramped muscles. Turning his head to the side, he opened his eyes and was nearly blinded by the beautiful, white light.

Lenore stared blankly at the circle of men gathered on the edge of the pit. Hettie had taken a position behind the coffee machine and found a niche fussing over the dejected rescue workers.

For several hours, heavy equipment had been removing the debris. The process had been painfully slow and Lenore suspected, dangerous. Beside her, Edison stood stoically but she could feel his tension as each massive beam was tenuously lifted from the rubble. One slip and—

Hettie suddenly appeared. "Drink this, dear. It will make you feel better."

Lenore listlessly accepted the foam cup and used it to warm her hands, belatedly murmuring her thanks. Hettie handed a second cup to Edison. Vaguely, Lenore was aware of her grandmother's concerned inquiry and Edison's terse response, but she was intently focused on the rescue activity and paid little attention to anything else.

Something was happening.

Acutely attuned to the subtlest change in the rescue rhythm, Lenore noticed that the workers' methodical efforts had become more urgent. The air was electric, charged by a sudden aura of immediacy that prickled her nape and tightened her chest.

Absently she took one step then another, oblivious to all but the excited voices of the workers and the tightly drawn cable extending into the excavation. Several men were leaning over the precipice, calling down to the workers below. The hoist squeaked, raising its cargo with unnerving hesitance. Lenore couldn't breathe. She dropped the still-full cup and moved forward, then felt a restraining hand on her arm. Pulling away, she stumbled, righted herself, then ran frantically across the rocky ground.

Workers shouted into the hole. The cable inched upward. Lenore ran faster.

The tip of a stretcher basket came into view, tilting a few feet beyond the waiting paramedics. Pandemonium broke out. People rushed from the control area. Medical personnel gathered equipment and dashed forward.

The hoist squeaked. The cable moved. The basket swung higher and higher and higher.

For Lenore, each breath was a tortured gasp as she willed her leaden legs to move faster. Someone was strapped to the basket, someone with shaggy black hair and a sharp, angled jaw. With a desperate cry, she propelled the final yards oblivious to the feel of the earth beneath her feet.

When the stretcher was finally pulled to safety, Lenore burst through the circle of medical personnel before her knees buckled. She collapsed, reaching out desperately,

"Steven!" Strong hands gripped her shoulder and she twisted away.

"*Steven!*"

The dark head turned. When she saw the crystal green eyes, lucid and obviously filled with life, a sob of relief caught in her throat. One arm was obviously injured but he extended the other and his lips silently formed her name. The anonymous hands held Lenore beyond his reach.

Finally she threw herself forward, flung both arms out and screamed his name. With a muttered curse, Steven struggled with the restraining strap.

A medic pressed him back, gesturing impatiently toward whoever was holding Lenore. Instantly, the pressure was gone and she crawled forward. When she reached Steven, she was both laughing and crying while her fingers frantically traced the rough contours of his body. He was real. He was whole.

"Steven," she whispered, thrilled by the sound of his name. She gently touched his bleeding head. "You're hurt."

"It's nothing." His eyes scanned her greedily, as though memorizing every nuance of her face.

Joyful tears blurred her view and she impatiently blinked them away. Without looking up, she spoke to the frustrated medic, who was trying to immobilize Steven's right arm. "How is he?"

"Vital signs are good," came the taut reply. Working quickly, the medic strapped a balloonlike contraption to Steven's injured wrist, then regarded Lenore kindly. "I could use a bit more room to finish checking him out."

Lenore was half sprawled across Steven's chest and had a death grip on his shirt. Still, she was reluctant to move away and looked up pleadingly.

Meanwhile Steven managed to unbuckle the restraining strap across his abdomen and struggled to sit up. "I'm okay," he mumbled but was unsuccessful in the gallant attempt to conceal a grimace. Sweat beaded his brow and his eyes glazed momentarily.

Instantly alarmed, Lenore slid an arm around his shoulders and eased him back to his prone position. "Please, let hem take care of you."

As she stood, Steven reached out and took her hand. Don't . . . leave."

"I won't." She gently kissed his bruised knuckles then rushed her cheek against his palm. "I love you, Steven."

His gaze didn't waver. "I know."

The quiet acknowledgement touched Lenore's heart. Jnable to trust her voice, she simply nodded, released his and and stepped back so the medics could continue their inistrations. She didn't know exactly when Edison had ppeared but realized that he was supporting both Lenore nd Hettie, with one lean arm around each of the women.

Absently chewing her lip, Lenore watched anxiously as teven's attention turned toward the fate of his crew. He was isibly relieved at learning that Chester and his foreman had ot been seriously injured, but his staid expression crumled when told that others had not been so fortunate. The orment in his eyes nearly ripped her heart out and only dison's firm grip kept Lenore from rushing to offer comort.

When the medic tried to start an IV, Steven sat upright nd swung his feet to the ground. "I don't need that," he rowled obstinately.

"Please, Mr. Collier, this is standard procedure. The mbulance is waiting—"

"I don't need any damned ambulance, either." With that, e was on his feet, swaying slightly.

Instantly Edison released the two women and stepped orward, simultaneously steadying Steven and speaking to e frustrated emergency worker. "We'll take care of him."

Lenore had followed Edison and now slid both arms ound Steven's waist, allowing him to lean on her while his ncle continued negotiations.

The thwarted medic stuffed a stethoscope into his breast ocket and eyed Edison with obvious frustration. "Look, e man's wrist is broken and he could have undetected in-

ternal injuries. In any case, he requires immediate medica
attention."

"We'll take him directly to the hospital," Edison replied
smoothly, then lowered his voice confidentially. "Steve
hates ambulances. It's a phobic thing. You can understand
that, can't you?"

"Well . . ."

"I'll take full responsibility," Edison added quickly.

"Actually he's in surprisingly good condition, all thing
considered." The medic shrugged, grabbed his case and
smiled at Steven. "Good luck, fella."

"I have plenty of that," Steven murmured, then gazed
down at Lenore while the paramedic disappeared into the
dispersing crowd.

Lenore touched her fingertips to the thick gauze taped to
Steven's forehead. "I thought I'd lost you."

"Never." Steven brushed one knuckle across her cheek
tracing the line of dried tears. When he spoke again, hi
voice was thick with emotion. "All those hours, I had time
to do some serious thinking—about life and death and al
that we take for granted. I realized that I was more afraid o
living than of dying."

Eyes wide, Lenore could only stammer. "You don't mean
that."

His thumb gently bushed her mouth, silencing her. "
couldn't control my feelings and I despised that weakness in
myself. I'd fallen in love with you and there wasn't on
damn thing I could do except deny it."

Lenore's legs trembled. *Love?* Had he actually said th
word or had she just imagined it? She would have asked
except her mouth was suddenly as dry as a desert.

Steven took a deep breath and closed his eyes. When h
opened them, he looked straight at her without a trace o
regret. "I love you, Lenore Gregory Blaine. That pit I wa
trapped in wasn't nearly as cold or dark or empty as my lif
would be if you weren't a part of it. I know that I'm n
prize, honey. I'm arrogant and stubborn and crabbier tha
hell when I don't get my own way and if you told me to dro

nchor off the coast of Timbuktu and never darken your
oor again, I'd understand— Am I rambling?''

Mouth agape, Lenore managed a limp nod.

''Sorry, it's just that I'm not very good at this sort of
ing.''

She found her voice. ''What sort of thing is that?''

He managed a strained smile. ''I'm supposed to kneel for
is but I'm afraid to turn you loose long enough to do that
here goes. I . . . want to marry you, Lenore. I want you to
e my wife.''

For several tense moments, Lenore couldn't speak.

Steven's expression tightened anxiously.

Then from behind them, Hettie spoke up impatiently.
For corn sake, child, say 'yes' or the poor man is going to
ave a stroke on the spot.''

Without taking her eyes from Steven's face, Lenore
hispered, ''Yes.''

He swallowed. ''Yes, you'll marry me?''

She smiled, stood on her tiptoes and confirmed her an-
ver with a sweet, slow kiss, then murmured, ''Does that
nswer your question?''

''I believe it does.'' Steven looked at Hettie and Edison,
ho were holding hands and grinning happily. ''She said
es.''

Edison nodded. ''So she did. Congratulations, son.''

''It's about time,'' Hettie pronounced. ''Kids today make
rerything so dadgummed difficult. Why, in my time—
/ell, never mind. I talk too much, don't I, Sonny?''

''Never, my sweet.''

Suddenly Lenore remembered the trip. Their flight left in
ss than two hours. ''Oh, Grandma, I'm sorry but I just
in't go to *Cabo* with you now.''

''Think nothing of it, dear.'' Hettie gazed up at Edison.
I think I can find another traveling companion.''

Steven's eyes narrowed. *''Cabo San Lucas?''*

''Yes. Grandma and I were supposed to leave this morn-
ig.''

"What a coincidence." Steven stared at his uncle. "Ed son and I had scheduled a fishing trip with the same dest nation."

"Really?" Lenore's gaze swung to her pink-faced grand mother. "Now that really *is* a coincidence, isn't it?"

Hettie shrugged happily. "Well, something had to b done. Everyone could see the two of you belonged togethe but Pisces and Cancer are such stubborn, independent sig that sometimes it just takes a little nudge, that's all. Sonn and I supplied the nudge. You two supplied the rest, rig dear?"

Edison cheerfully agreed. "You *are* stubborn, Steve Always have been, ever since you were a tight-mouthe kid."

Lenore spoke up. "So you two conspired to set Steven an I up with a romantic, south-of-the-border rendezvous an this business about you and Edison getting a divorce was a part of the ploy, wasn't it?"

"Of course it was." Hettie seemed mightily offende "Why, you don't think I'd let a prize like Sonny go withou a fight, do you? Now if you two hadn't been so pigheade Sonny and I never would have had to stoop to such a d ception. Still, everything worked out quite nicely, don't yo think?"

Lenore didn't answer. Instead she gazed mistily int Steven's forest-green eyes and realized the near-tragedy ha opened her heart and mind to one simple truth: To fear lov was to fear life itself.

And for the first time in years, Lenore was not afraid.

Epilogue

teven leaned over his drafting table and absently watched
arks of sunlight skipping across rolling blue swells. The
eanfront apartment had been a good compromise. Of
urse, the past eight months had seen many such compro-
ises and incalculable other changes. Steven smiled se-
ely, content with himself and his new life. He could
member every detail of his old existence but those days
emed detached, as though lived by someone else. He
asn't the same man. He was happy.

The front door opened and his heart leaped like a trout.
tch instantly arose from his nap and plodded into the
ing room, tail wagging.

She was home. Her soft footsteps were muted by carpet-
g but Steven's ears were finely attuned to every nuance of
s wife's presence. His first instinct was to jump up and
eep her into his arms, filling his soul with the feel and the
ent and the taste of her sweetness.

But he didn't want to display eagerness, didn't want her
recognize the frightening depth of his emotion. Not that
e was deceived, of course. That sweet, knowing smile told
even that she was wise to his ploy and understood that a

man with a guarded soul had to remove the armor slowly
piece by piece. Part of him still waited for the fairy tale t
end. Part of him knew that it never would.

She called his name. The sound of her voice thrilled hir
and joyful sparks skittered down his spine.

"I'm in the office, honey." He was pleased by his nor
chalant reply but as he greedily listened to the soft foot
steps, he clutched the arms of his swivel chair to keep fror
grabbing her when she appeared.

Suddenly she was there, rushing through the doorwa
with windblown hair and flushed cheeks. "I picked up th
mail and there's a letter from Grandma and Edison! It'
postmarked Jakarta. That's in Java, isn't it?" Withou
awaiting an answer, Lenore hurried across the roon
plopped on Steven's lap and wiggled the envelope in fror
of him. "I can't believe they actually had the courage to d
this. I could understand a weekend in Catalina, but bor
rowing that pitiful old boat for a six-month cruise to Indc
nesia, now there's an act of faith."

"Edison is a fine sailor and I'll have you know that th
Bohemian is still every bit as seaworthy as the day she wa
launched."

Ignoring Steven's feigned indignation, Lenore squirme
impatiently. To tease her, Steven made a production c
opening the envelope and held the letter away from her ex
cited eyes and peered inside. "Hmm. Pictures."

"Oh, let me see!" As she lunged for the precious enve
lope, Steven held it over his head, beyond her reach. He
eyes flashed adorably. "Hand it over," she warned, "or I'
bite your nose."

He grinned lecherously. "Promises, promises." When sh
ominously bared her teeth, he relented and gave her th
photos.

Instantly she arranged them across the drafting tab!
while Steven read the enclosed letter. Or tried to read it. L
nore suddenly shook his arm and squeaked with delight.

"Look, Grandma's actually wearing a bathing suit! Isn
that a kick? And Edison looks ten years younger. Goo
grief, he's as brown as a nut."

Steven glanced at the photo in question. "Travel must gree with them. They've never looked better."

With a wistful sigh, Lenore snuggled against Steven's hest and listened quietly as he read Edison's letter aloud. ach paragraph described daring exploits and exotic lo- als. Steven's pulse raced and he conjured images of dupli- ating the colorful journey. It would be glorious, the dventure of a lifetime.

By the time he read the affectionate postscript, Steven had apped a mental itinerary and was so wrapped up in the xciting prospect that he didn't notice Lenore had become ncharacteristically quiet.

"They're having the time of their lives," Steven pro- ounced enthusiastically. "They're going to be back in a ouple of months but it seems a shame to let the *Bohemian* nguish at a dock when there are so many wonderful places see."

"Umm." Lenore sat up and rubbed her stomach.

"What do you say, honey? The downtown project is fi- ally completed and I could use a few months off. We could lan our own cruise—Tahiti, maybe, or Samoa. I had a iend once who spent an entire summer on Fiji and— Le- ore? What's wrong?"

Lenore had suddenly stood and was grasping her abdo- en with apparent distress. Without responding to his con- rned inquiry, she whirled and rushed to the bathroom.

Although Steven knew Lenore wasn't all that fond of oats, her reaction seemed a bit extreme. Besides, over the ast months they had come to a rather amiable agreement: teven would learn how to follow a trail and recognize poi- n oak; Lenore would buy a case of Dramamine and give ating a second chance.

Confused, Steven followed and cautiously tapped on the osed door. In reply, he heard the faucets turned on at full ast. "I'm willing to compromise, here," he called out. We could try a couple of short trips first, just until you get ur sea legs."

The water stopped and after a moment, Lenore opened e door. She was pale and obviously weak. Alarmed by her

wan appearance, Steven slipped an arm around her wais
and helped her to the sofa. "I'm going to call the doctor,"
he announced.

"I'm fine."

"You're not fine. You're as white as a ghost." Ignorin
her protest, Steven grabbed the telephone receiver and sup
pressed growing panic. "I'm calling 911."

Lenore pushed herself upright. "Don't be ridiculous
That number is for real emergencies."

"You're sick. That *is* a real emergency."

Patiently Lenore pried the telephone receiver from Ste
ven's grasp and cradled it. "I'm perfectly healthy, my love
Unfortunately, your plans for an oceanic adventure wi
have to be put on hold for a year or so."

A vague awareness tickled Steven's brain but at the mo
ment, he was much too befuddled to analyze the odd sen
sation. "Why?"

Smiling, she caressed his cheek with her fingertip. "Be
cause we'll have to wait until the baby is old enough for wa
ter wings. Safety first, you know. It shouldn't be all tha
long. Two years at the most. He or she will be walking b
then, so we'll have to do something about reinforcing thos
guardrails. Maybe some kind of netting or we might be abl
to—Steven? Darling, are you all right?"

"Baby?" he croaked, steadying himself on the sofa arm
Lenore smiled sweetly. "Yes, dear."

Steven blinked frantically. "A baby person?"

Lenore's smile faded. "Well, hopefully..."

"You mean diapers and bottles and walking the floor a
night?" Oblivious to Lenore's stunned expression, Steve
whirled and paced the living room, rubbing his neck mu
tering. "Cribs and car seats and high chairs and a colleg
fund—" He lurched to a stop, spun and took two broa
steps, then dropped to his knees in front of the sofa. Lif
ing Lenore's hand, he anxiously scanned her startled fac
"Are you all right? Do you need anything? Milk. Yo
should drink lots of milk. And vitamins. You have to tak
those special mommy vitamins, don't you? Have you see

doctor? Never mind. We'll go right now. Don't get up. I'll carry you."

Before he could stand, Lenore leaned forward and framed his face with her hands. She gently kissed his mouth, then searched his eyes with an odd, wistful expression that made his heart ache. "Are you happy, Steven? I don't just mean about the baby. I mean are you happy with me...with us?"

For a moment, he was too overcome to even move. How could she ask? Didn't she know how precious she was to him? Unable to speak, he turned his face and gently kissed her palm. When he looked up again, she was smiling.

Taking his beloved wife in his arms, Steven closed his eyes and offered a silent salute to the spirited seniors who had taught them the greatest lesson of all.

It's never too late for love.

* * * * *

LOVE AND
THE CANCER MAN

by Wendy Corsi Staub

July starts off with a bang on Independence Day, and the home-loving patriotic Cancer man likes nothing better than to celebrate with a backyard barbecue. After sundown, he'll want to cuddle with his sweetheart on a blanket beneath the stars to watch a dazzling fireworks display. He has a deep appreciation for beauty and romance, so the brilliant explosions in the sky are likely to ignite a more intimate glow between the Cancer man and his mate!

In THE LAST BACHELOR, Cancer man Steven Collier can't help being starry-eyed over outgoing Pisces woman Lenore Blaine, whose animated personality keeps him fascinated. What special something creates sparks between the Cancer man and YOU?

The *Aries* woman's boundless energy often causes the Cancer man to sit back in awe. He's filled with wonder over the way she manages to accomplish ten things at once—and rarely appear winded! The Aries woman, meanwhile, finds the Cancer man a sensitive, considerate lover who manages to make her see that taking *some* things slowly can be appealing!

The *Taurus* woman, once she's fallen for the Cancer man, will tend to dote on him, and he revels in her attention othing is too good for her man—breakfast in bed, steaming bubble baths—and she knows how to keep him coming back for more. All he needs is lots of love, and all she needs is someone to shower with affection. This can be an ideal relationship!

The *Gemini* woman is a thinker. Her clever mind will always hold the Cancer man's rapt attention. These two can have real conversations, and the Cancer man finds his mate a endless supply of worthwhile information. But the Cancer man likes to *feel*, too, and the Gemini woman can't help but respond to his deep desire for love.

When the Cancer man joins forces with a *Cancer* woman, the match is bound to result in a mutual admiration society. Their biggest focus in life is on their home, and they'll make it a lovely, cozy retreat where they'll spend as much time as possible alone together. They share a variety of domestic talents, and are likely to team up for lots of gourmet cooking, remodeling and decorating.

It was probably love at first sight for the Cancer man and *Leo* woman. She knows how to dazzle, and he's a great admirer of all kinds of beauty! She finds that he is first-rate husband material—he'll make her his first priority, and nothing could make the Leo lady happier than a lifetime of adoration.

The Cancer man finds the shy, sweet *Virgo* woman irresistible. He'll want to break down her protective walls, piece by piece, and make her feel warmth and trust. She'll let him in...eventually. His romantic soul and sensitive nature make him a risk worth taking. Besides, he needs *her* love, too—and she'll gladly give it.

The *Libra* woman and the Cancer man are sensitive, emotional individuals. They appreciate this about each other, and find it attractive. They're both somewhat insecure, so

they'll recognize this in their partner and go out of their wa
to offer loving encouragement and support...just when it'
needed most!

Few matches in the zodiac are as suited as the Cancer ma
and the *Scorpio* woman. He loves to be nurtured, and sh
likes nothing better than to do the nurturing. She can b
fiercely jealous, but he's secretly flattered—and so devote
she'll never have to worry. These two are destined to liv
happily ever after!

The vivacious *Sagittarius* woman is the life of every party
and the Cancer man can't help being drawn to her easygo
ing, fun-loving nature. She knows how to have a goo
time—especially with her attentive Cancer escort at her side
She'll always find him an excellent mate—passionate, loya
and sensitive. What more could she ask?

The Cancer man can be a warrior now and then, and the
sensible *Capricorn* woman is just the person to make him se
there's nothing to fret about. He'll marvel at her ability t
be straightforward and logical even when times are tough
And she'll be touched by his desire to be a sound pro
vider...the traditional breadwinner and head of his fam
ily.

The Cancer man and the *Aquarius* woman are a classic ex
ample of opposites attracting. These two have polar view
points on most issues, from politics to daily routines—yet
that's what keeps life interesting! As long as they're to
gether, there's bound to be occasional bursts of fireworks...
but making up afterward is always glorious!

Silhouette
R O M A N C E™

NEW COVER
Coming this September

The Silhouette woman is ever changing, and now we're changing, too.

Silhouette Romance has a new look, but inside you'll find the same heartwarming, satisfying love stories that emphasize the traditional values of family, commitment...and the special kind of love that is destined to last forever.

Look for the new Silhouette Romance cover this September.

When it comes to passion, we wrote the book.

NORA ROBERTS

Love has a language all its own, and for centuries, flowers have symbolized love's finest expression. Discover the language of flowers—and love—in this romantic collection of 48 favorite books by bestselling author Nora Roberts.

Two titles are available each month at your favorite retail outlet.

In July, look for:

Search for Love, **Volume #11**
Playing the Odds, **Volume #12**

In August, look for:

Tempting Fate, **Volume #13**
From this Day, **Volume #14**

Collect all 48 titles
and become fluent in

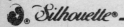

BIG SUMMER READ

Summer Reading At Its Best

In July, Harlequin and Silhouette bring readers the Big Summer Read Program. Heat up your summer with these four exciting new novels by top Harlequin and Silhouette authors.

SOMEWHERE IN TIME by Barbara Bretton
YESTERDAY COMES TOMORROW by Rebecca Flanders
A DAY IN APRIL by Mary Lynn Baxter
LOVE CHILD by Patricia Coughlin

From time travel to fame and fortune, this program offers something for everyone.

Available at your favorite retail outlet.

BSR

WRITTEN IN THE STARS

WHEN A LEO MAN MEETS A GEMINI WOMAN

Seth Danner's daughter was the single most important thing in his life—until he hired beautiful, vibrant Margo Rourke as his new housekeeper. But Seth had no way of knowing that Margo's secret might destroy his family....

Will the power of love bring these people together? Find out in Suzanne Carey's BABY SWAP—the **WRITTEN IN THE STARS** title for August 1992. Only from Silhouette Romance!

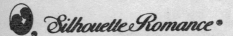